Y0-BZZ-906

Miners' Moon

A NELLIE BURNS AND MOONSHINE MYSTERY

MINERS' MOON

JULIE WESTON

FIVE STAR
A part of Gale, a Cengage Company

LIBRARY OF CONGRESS CATALOGING-IN-PUBLICATION DATA

Names: Weston, Julie W., 1943– author.
Title: Miners' moon / Julie Weston.
Description: First Edition. | Waterville, Maine : Five Star, a part of Gale, a Cengage Company, 2021. | Series: A Nellie Burns and moonshine mystery
Identifiers: LCCN 2021022275 | ISBN 9781432888046 (hardcover)
Subjects: GSAFD: Mystery fiction.
Classification: LCC PS3623.E872 M56 2021 | DDC 813/.6—dc23

First Edition. First Printing: December 2021
Find us on Facebook—https://www.facebook.com/FiveStarCengage
Visit our website—http://www.gale.cengage.com/fivestar
Contact Five Star Publishing at FiveStar@cengage.com

Printed in Mexico
Print Number: 01 Print Year: 2022

For Gerry, as always

ACKNOWLEDGMENTS

Mining began in north Idaho in the 1880s and continued for over 100 years. The largest mine, which I call the Gem Mining Company, lasted to 1980 when it was shut down for environmental problems. It opened briefly in 1990 and 1991 and may again open in the future. Nearly all of the other mines in the Silver Valley, as it is now called, have been closed as well. One or two continue to operate, although not at the level they once did.

I descended into the largest mine while researching the book I eventually wrote about the Idaho mining town where I grew up: *The Good Times Are All Gone Now: Life, Death and Rebirth in an Idaho Mining Town* (University of Oklahoma Press, 2009). I was given a tour beginning at the entry level, down into one of the active stopes where men mined for lead and silver, and deeper to the lowest level of the mine. I felt every inch of the mountain above me the whole time. But I also saw the possibility for a murder mystery in some of the workings. When I embarked on the Moon books and Nellie Burns, I remembered one place in particular and have always planned for its use.

My writing colleagues have once again critiqued and made suggestions for this Moon book. I thank Belinda Anderson, Mary Murfin Bayley, and Tony Tekaroniake Evans for their insightful comments and assistance.

The IDAHO Magazine has always provided background information about Idaho and in particular an article by Mike

Blackbird, a regular contributor, about Burke, Idaho. For anyone curious about Idaho towns and history, this magazine is well worth the subscription.

My *Good Times* book also detailed some of the union problems that always seemed to plague the Silver Valley. I called upon my experiences then and many articles and several books about union strife in Idaho in writing this story. Besides my own trip into the mine, I used *Fire in the Hole: The Untold Story of Hardrock Miners* (WSU Press, 1994) by Jerry Dolph and *Rock Burst* (University of Idaho Press, 1998) by Bert Russell and Marie Russell to provide some specific details about mining.

My author's note at the end lists other people and information that informed my writing for this book for which I am grateful. Any errors in geology, mining, bootlegging, and photography are mine.

The pandemic slowed progress on this book and many others at the publisher, Five Star Publishing, for a period of six months. Thanks to Tiffany Schofield, Acquisitions Editor, for re-establishing the process toward publication and for choosing this story of another foundation of Idaho's history. Thanks also to Hazel Rumney, developmental editor extraordinaire, for her assistance. Elizabeth Trupin-Pulli, my able agent, has been encouraging and helpful to me with this fourth mystery.

As always, I thank my husband, Gerry Morrison, for his photography expertise in large format cameras. He has the patience of a loving husband, and I return the loving in equal measure.

Chapter One

Blood oozed like liquid glue down the side of the mine sled. Men, some scorched, others gashed, were tied to the sled walls so they wouldn't slip and fall down the shaft. As if they weren't dead, or nearly so, already. A few others sat up, their hands gripping the sides, their eyes glowing white surrounded by dirt or oil. Their faces were set in the rictus of death, and yet their hands moved, their heads turned.

"How many are coming up?" Nellie Burns glanced around the tunnel where she stood with Sheriff Asteguigoiri, her boss from her home in central Idaho. Lights glared near the cable hauling in the mine sled, but the outer edges of the carved-out room in the mine felt threatening.

They watched the man-sled pull up the main shaft to Level Nine, the mine's entrance level, where they stood. She wanted to turn away, but it was her job to take photographs with her large format Premo camera, her almost constant companion.

The cable creaked as it wrapped around a giant drum at the far end of the room. The heavy counterweight in the shaft sank down to what some thought was the pit of hell, but the supervisors called the lowest working level of the Gem Company mine. Even the smell of sulfur confirmed they might be dealing with the subject of one of Dante's circles.

Nellie stepped aside to throw up, relieved to be wearing pants and not a dress. She cleaned her face with her handkerchief and returned to Sheriff Charlie's side.

"I don't know. Tying the victims from the explosion to the sled must take time. Are you all right?" Charlie asked.

Nell nodded, steadied her camera on its tripod, covered her head with the black cloth, focused on the tableau, pulled off the cloth, slid in the film holder, pulled out the dark slide, and waited to open the lens while she signaled to the deputy assisting her. He held the phosphorus in a tray ready to light. She lowered her hand. *Pfloosh.* Like lightning, the powder exploded, white light filled the cave, and she closed the lens. The circle of hell was now imprinted on film, a record of what they saw that day in the mine.

Groans combined with shouts from the ambulance crews helping men out of the sled. Open ore cars, empty of rock, lined the tracks back to the outside, waiting for injured miners. Nellie saw that silent bodies were piled in one of the last cars. No hurry for its departure. The now empty sled dropped down the shaft, a silent disappearance. How many more times would it bring out victims?

After three additional photographs, and when no more men appeared from the depths, she hopped onto a smaller, flatter car, like a railroad jitney, that the sheriff flagged for her. She was so relieved to leave the mine, she didn't even thank him, just stepped on, holding her equipment close to her bosom.

After Nellie left the scene of burnt miners behind, she felt as if she had escaped from the devil. The smelter smoke outside was a relief from singed skin and burnt hair. Even though she had spent less than a full day inside the mine workings photographing the horror, the time had slowed until the sense of the dark underground had merged into one long Lucifer's night.

The sun sank toward the mountains, draining color from the bare areas of the mountain slopes opposite the mine entrance, the north side of the valley. The dirt stretches looked like so many scabrous patches of leprosy, surrounded by deep-green evergreens that would soon be eaten up and swallowed by the gluttonous maw of the adit, the mine entrance. She shook herself, lifted her camera bag to her shoulder, and began to trudge up the street to the uptown hotel. A bath and a nap might ease the pain of being a police photographer. Maybe she could even spend time later with her camera and brighter, lighter subjects.

As she walked, the mountains loomed around her. She found herself hunching from the strain of carrying the memory of inside the mine on her shoulders, just as she had felt there, aware of every level of earth above her. The contrast between this town and the south central Idaho area she now called home was stark, especially the sagebrush mountains around Hailey and Ketchum. This silver valley spread almost the same width as her adopted home in the Big Wood River valley. There, her eyes lifted to light and sun. Photographing became a challenge to find the right subject to place under the long view, under the ever-blooming clouds, lit by the favorable light. Dusk lasted a long time, and a vanilla cast to the sun intensified shadows, turned colors to their complements. Here, the sun hardly seemed to rise before its descent toward mountains and darkness, an exaggeration of course, but seeming to mimic the hard life of miners.

Her camera grew heavier as she approached the hotel, rumored to have women of the night in several rooms—soiled doves, as she had heard. That was certainly like Hailey. Mining and sheepherding served as local support, she gathered. She ruminated on taking photos of the women. If for no other reason, those portraits would be interesting because of the stories behind them. She wondered if the sheriff would object. She would use her own film, not the county's.

As if conjured by her thoughts, he appeared behind her and

opened the hotel door. This man, this Basque sheriff, an anomaly in itself, this former sheepherder, was the man she worked for—his crime photographer.

"We must talk," he said in his slightly accented speech, a holdover from the Euskara language of his youth. "Alone. This situation is more complicated than the local authorities told the state police office."

Nellie nodded, wishing her camera pack were lighter. Charlie lifted it from her shoulders and shepherded her into a small private meeting room off the main lobby. Nell plunked herself down in a chair faded to beige stained with cigar smoke. She could even smell the sour odor and would have sworn she could taste it. Her clothes must smell of sulfur from the mine—her pants, her jacket. She had pulled a hat on and stuffed her hair into it. She must look like a man, a small one. She jerked the hat off and shook her head to let her hair fly loose, relieved it was now only past her ears.

"Are you all right, Nell?" Charlie didn't wait for an answer. "You look exhausted, and no wonder. That mine accident could cut out the heart of a strong man. When the local police asked me to go down and see what was going on, I did not know it would be like that." The sheriff paced. "Otherwise, I would not have taken you with me. Worse, it was no accident."

"What do you mean?" The horror she had felt in the mine threatened her gorge again.

"Someone—a miner, a superintendent—someone set off the dynamite and started the fire in the lower level. One of the burned men brought up a petrol can. He said the fire exploded right next to him. He was hurt, but crawled to the hoist and signaled for a pickle barrel and relayed the fire alert."

"But, but—how did the man get out? What is a pickle barrel?" More questions came, but she held them in.

"The sled that men ride down into the mine and up again."

The sheriff pulled an equally greasy, armless chair from the conference table and sat astride, as if on a horse.

"How do you know this man didn't do it?" She straightened in her chair, the better to think.

"We don't. He died. The company official who confirmed his tale said every single man who came out could have done it. So could any super or anyone else who had a grudge. He wants to blame it on the union—said he'll call Pinkerton and get a private detective here."

"Then we can go home." Ketchum never felt so dear.

"We're supposed to investigate the scheme to violate the Prohibition laws and possibly a federal murder as we talked about on the way here, not this mine accident. That mine fire was just a diversion for us. We are involved because we happened to be in town."

A good clean murder seemed a relief. "What about the local police? I still don't understand why we were called in."

"Remember the moonshine operation near Stanley?"

"How could I forget? My arm still feels stiff." She lifted her left forearm. Days like today brought on a deep ache, as if the knife were still inside. "And I do remember that you arrested me." She smiled briefly at him and noticed his blush.

He ducked his head, reached toward her but then dropped his arm. He continued. "This murder may involve bootlegging and mining both. The federal marshal thinks the local police and city officials may be involved. The police do not know we are investigating them as well. Otherwise, I do not think the police chief would have asked for my help. We need a trustworthy miner to go down, work shifts, get close. Maybe we'll solve both crimes." His broad shoulders had slumped, but, as he talked, he straightened up again.

"How about Rosy? Does he still know how to mine?" Rosy was her friend from her first days in Ketchum, a miner no longer. His blind eye could be a handicap, but Nell didn't want to bring that up.

"Maybe. One does not forget sheepherding, and one does not forget mining. But no one can know, and he does not exactly keep his mouth closed."

"He's better." She smiled. Rosy would do anything he said he would do, but he was ornery.

"You can wire him at Western Union. Say you need him to help find your uncle."

"My uncle? What uncle?"

Chapter Two

"Are you Basque?"

"Yes. I wonder how you could tell." Few people outside Hailey and Ketchum even knew what Basque were. Most people thought Charlie was Mexican, not a favored group in Idaho. The same was true of Negroes. He wore his county sheriff's badge on his jacket.

"There's a Basque boardinghouse up the road a piece in Mullan—that's where the Morning Mine is. I worked with Basque who stay there." The miner talking to Charlie was short and barrel chested, as well as clean shaven, maybe one of the immigrants who came to Bitterroot to work in the Gem mine, where the explosion took place.

"Never seen a Basque copper before, though." The man laughed, gestured toward the badge, and his chest shook. That action spurred a bout of coughing. Finally, he stopped and could talk. "You here to collar them bootleggers? They're selling poison. A better bet is the Dago wine them I-talians make." He used an "I" for the ethnic group, something everyone in Gem did, not with rancor, but as the normal course. "My name is Izzie Savich. I been here a long time now. Know about ever'one. I'm Croat myself."

The two of them sat together at a counter in the café next door to the Callahan Hotel. Nell Burns hadn't shown her face yet—early hours didn't seem to be her usual practice. When she did show up, she nodded at the Croat and Charlie and sat at a table, not the counter.

"That is Miss Burns. She is a police photographer," Charlie said. "You peg me on both counts. Basque and a law man." He lifted his hand to shake the miner's. "I'm Charlie Asteguigoiri, usually called Charlie Azgo. It appears I will be helping with the explosion in the mine. Know anything about it?"

"Nah. I didn't work yesterday. Got my friend Mustard to pull a double shift for me, poor sod. I gotta bad leg. Doc told me to rest up a few days." Izzie sipped from a cup of black coffee. He acknowledged Nell with a wave of his hand, then turned his back on her. "He owed me, but didn't deserve to be kilt. Leastwise not that way." He took another sip and began coughing again.

Charlie said nothing, waiting for more. Most people felt the need to fill a silence.

"Burned. One of the first to come up, I heard. Mine people thought it was me. He was single and a bit of a loner. Married man myself." He shook his head. "Or was. She died on me a while back. Kids grown, but I'm still a family man. Not like Mustard—the guy who died. Izzie and Mustard. Quite the pair we are—were. We could win any double jack contest—and did. Don't know who'll turn the hand drill with me at the Miners Picnic this year." His countenance looked as if he had lost his best friend.

Charlie waited a moment, then asked, "Who do you think did it?"

"Blew up the dynamite? Coulda been a accident, you know."

"Yes. It could have been." He could feel Nell listening from the table behind them.

"Don't think so, though. Wrong place." Cough, cough.

"Wrong place?"

"Ain't no dynamite stored near there—no drilling there, neither. Might could be a fire, I s'pose, but nothin' to blow up like that, except someone planned it and detonated some sticks right where the muckers waited to go out at the end of the shift. They was lucky the cable didn't get broke. Would've closed the mine down." His look had turned hopeful.

Charlie kept his face as still as he could, his stone face as Nell called it. He wanted to ask Izzie how he knew so much about the explosion but didn't want to scare him quiet. He waited but made an encouraging sound. "Hmmmm."

" 'Course, I only know what I heard from the muckers that made it out. Could be I'm wrong. I'd blame Gem, though. They're ham handed and don't take care of the men the way they should." He shrugged. "Better'n Butte, though, I've heard."

"Any mucker in particular?"

"Let's see. Maki and Tater were hurt but not bad. Maki was comin' in on a skip 'cause he's a skip-tender." Izzie stood up from the bar seat, none too steady. "Tater was back from the sled run. Gotta go see a man about a horse." He glanced at Nellie and limped off, coughing.

The sheriff joined Nellie at the table. "There is a Basque boardinghouse up the road," he said, "according to that man, Izzie Savich. I want to visit it."

"He sounded ill with all that coughing. Was he all right?"

"It could be miners' con—consumption. A lot of the men suffer from it when they have been underground too long."

The two of them walked up the main street after breakfast. Charlie felt hemmed in by the steep hillsides of the town. Nell didn't seem bothered. She even commented that the mountains looked down the same as the tall buildings in Chicago. Charlie flinched from the sense that the sides might cave in on him, the same dread he had suffered inside the mine. He would be happy to delay going back in. "I will ask to borrow an automobile from the police chief here, so we can go east to Mullan."

"How will that get us answers to what is going on here?" Nellie looked up at Charlie. She always seemed so petite to him that he had to keep himself from patting her head, but that would be anathema to her determination to be a proper professional.

"The federal marshal said something is going on in that town with bootleggers and, uh, ladies of the night, as well as local town fathers. Liquor flows as if there were not a Prohibition at all. Maybe we can find a loquacious Basque." Or someone Charlie might know from his sheepherding days.

Nellie trilled a laugh, an almost bird-song sound. She put her arm through Charlie's. "Let's go. I want to meet a loquacious Basque. I doubt if there is such a person in the wide world."

They waited until late afternoon, while the sheriff visited the mine offices, and Nell sent off a telegram to Rosy and walked around town. She took her camera and photographed business signs, the mine entrance, and a building identified as the rock house by a stranger. Charlie borrowed an automobile without town markings on it. It might be useful to be anonymous, Nell had pointed out. She had dithered about whether to wear her pants or a dress. Be a man or a woman. She settled on the latter and felt lighter because of it. Her skirt was not as short as she had seen in some magazines, and, indeed, right there in Bitterroot, but she definitely approved of shorter hems over the longer, constricting clothes once in fashion. How had her mother and her friends stood it? If nothing else, the War to End All Wars had changed fashion for once and all.

In the late afternoon, they drove east along the river, flowing in the opposite direction with its grayish cast reflecting the pewter clouds or carrying mine tailings, Nell wasn't sure. As they approached Wallace, she saw where a huge fire had burned trees off the hillsides more than a decade before. Only small seedlings grew now, but, maybe one day, they would be a forest again. A large building stood across the river, apparently unburned. They wound past the town with its many brick buildings and some empty spaces where structures used to stand. Farther east, the forests grew thick and green, and the air smelled of the tall ponderosa pine and cedar, trees she only had a nodding acquaintance with. Another mile or two and they arrived at a small town with houses edging up at least one gulch, maybe more. There were fewer brick buildings and more wood ones, except for what looked like a concrete building. "I wonder what that is," she mused out loud. As they neared, she could see the letters The Morning Club on it.

Charlie drove as if he knew where they were going and proceeded to get lost. At the end of a narrow gulch with neat frame houses, he turned around.

"Stop! I'll ask directions." Nell wound her window down as they pulled up to a woman working in a garden. "Do you know where the Basque boardinghouse is?"

The woman stood up, wiping her hands on an apron obviously used for that purpose several times. "Eh?"

"The Basque boardinghouse? We seem to be lost."

The woman wore braids wrapped around her head. She nodded and said, "Back down that way. Big house on the right. Big yard. No flowers." Her Scandinavian accent was strong. She smiled and nodded again. "Basque good people." She ducked her head to look past Nellie at the sheriff. "You Basque?"

Charlie looked discomfited. Nellie said, "Yes." Before she rolled up her window, she thanked the woman.

The house was indeed big, three possibly four stories, and painted white with red trim. She wondered how they missed it on their way up the gulch. Over the front door with its oval window, a red, green, and white sign announced something in what Nellie imagined must be Euskara. She asked Charlie.

"*Ostatuak*. Boardinghouse. This is it. I am surprised we did not see it traveling up the road."

"I didn't know to look for it. Even if I had, I don't think I would have recognized it for a boardinghouse sign. It looks quiet. Maybe everyone is at work."

Her companion made a sound, like a snorted laugh. "We will see."

Even as they walked up a narrow stone walkway, Nellie could smell cooking garlic and onions. She pulled in a deep breath, almost tasting the combination. It was such a wonderful contrast to the smelter smoke in Bitterroot, she wanted more of it. Charlie tapped on the door and then opened it. The cooking smells intensified and broadened. Nellie recognized the aroma of roasting lamb and rosemary. It was as if she were back in the Stanley Basin and her sheepherder friend Alphonso was preparing mutton stew after a long day in the mountains with the sheep. "It smells like home," she whispered to Charlie. Even his face had relaxed into a satisfied expression.

Inside the front door was a small entry opening out into a large living area, except no one was "living" in it. Instead there were three card tables, each with four men all playing cards. The room was almost silent except for the shuffling of cards and single cards passed around like whispers. Then shoulders lifted, arms stretched, eyes winked, and hands scratched necks. She jumped when a man shouted from one of the tables.

Nell did not understand what was going on, but Charlie had hurried over to one of the tables, a grin on his face. He exchanged a handshake of sorts with one of the men who sat next to another man with a bandaged head and one arm in a sling. All the men had long ear lobes and the same dark coloring Charlie did—black hair and dark eyes. They were uniformly handsome.

A woman, also dark and handsome but stocky, came through a swinging door with a tray of cups filled with something other than coffee, it appeared. Nellie surmised it was either whiskey or cider. The woman set a cup down beside each man. Charlie introduced himself in Euskara. She answered in English, smiling as she slightly bowed. "Ah, another Basko. You are welcome here. Are you looking for a room?" She glanced at Nellie and returned her gaze to the sheriff.

"No, we heard there was a Basque boardinghouse here in Mullan, and I wanted to see it. It has been a while since I have visited such a place," he said, "and seen a group of *mus* players. Do you have a *pelota* square outside as well?"

"We do not. The mountain rises too steep behind us," she said. "My name is Lorea. My husband, Dominic, and I own this house. We come from Biskaia. Do you?"

"Yes. My mother continues to live there, along with a brother and a sister. My father died in one of the battles between France and Spain some years ago. I live now in Hailey, Idaho, another mining town. I knew Mikel there," he said and placed his hand on the shoulder of the *mus* player he had greeted, "while sheepherding in the Stanley Basin, north of Hailey."

Lorea turned to Nellie. "Are you Basko, too? You do not look it." She stepped nearer and took a closer look, especially at Nellie's hair and then dress.

"I shouldn't wonder. I'm Nellie Burns from Chicago. I am a photographer and wanted to get photographs of the miners and others in this area. Usually, I focus on landscapes, but I think people subjects are much more appealing in many ways, especially to art studios." Nellie turned to face the card players again and swept her arm around. "I would like to photograph these men. Do you think they'd mind? Do they do this every day? I would think they would be exhausted after working in a mine all day."

The woman laughed, a laugh that included her whole face. "None of them are too tired to gamble and drink." Lorea glanced toward Charlie and said to both of them, "Please stay for dinner. It is lamb stew and will be ready soon. You can ask about pictures then." She passed back through the swinging door, still chuckling.

Charlie's friend, Mikel, rose from his table where the men were putting the cards away. "Charlie! It is good to see you, even if you have changed your name. Does no one call you Carlos anymore?" His wide grin showed crooked, white teeth. He was not quite as tall as Charlie, and his hair hung to his collar in back, but, otherwise, he could have been a brother.

The man with the sling and bandage stood as well with the cup in his hand and hovered nearby. "You're two sheepherders? How come everyone calls 'em maggots?"

"Not everyone does. Only cowboys and cattle ranchers," Charlie said. "Are you a cowboy? Fall off a horse?"

"Nah. I got caught in that hellfire in the mine. Oops, sorry little lady." He bowed low and swept what appeared to be a beret off the back of his head with his free hand. "I'd rather herd sheep any day than go back down into that sinkhole." He replaced his beret into a slaunchways position on his head. It didn't cover the bandage, but did give him a Frenchy look. "I'm Txomin." He slurped from his cup and set it down on a side table.

Nellie heard the name as "cho-men." She thought he sounded as if he had been drinking, but he didn't smell like alcohol. "Pleased to meet you both," she said. Txomin shook Charlie's hand. All four stood with no conversation for a moment or two. Txomin gestured to the other card players. "They'll be done soon. Then we can eat. No one's making any money. Not like me." He put his hand in his pocket and pulled out a sheaf of bills. "Soon's I make enough, I'm going back to Spain. Had enough of this mucky place."

"Did you see the explosion?" Charlie asked. "Know how it

happened?"

"Some piss—oops, sorry again. Some . . . ," he said but couldn't come up with a name. "The company wanted to get rid of union members. They're usually first to the man-car, so a turncoat set off a load of dynamite. I ain't one of 'em. I'm just a mucker, not like Mikel here. He's a powderman. He coulda done it for all I know. Except he doesn't work there." He punched his companion in the arm, softly, and growled a low sound, maybe a laugh, maybe not.

The ring of a bell sounded from beyond where Lorea had disappeared. "Dinner's on," Mikel said. He ignored Txomin and ushered Charlie and Nellie into the dining room with a table set for more than a dozen. Alongside it was a narrow serving buffet with a huge platter of mashed potatoes, a tureen full of lamb stew, another platter of green beans and cooked carrots, a third with what looked like red peppers, rolls with butter, a wriggling dish of orange Jell-O, and a stack of cookies almost ready to fall over. No wonder it is called a groaning board, she thought. The men waited for her, so she went first, trying not to load her dinner plate too full to leave room for a cookie at the end.

Lorea sat at the head of the table and kept her eye on everything—the men, the food, Nellie, Charlie, the pitcher of the brown liquid, the salt and pepper, the passing dish of sweet red peppers. When everyone's mouth was full, she piped up. "Nell Burns here wants to take your picture playing *mus*. Anyone object? No? Good. That's settled."

A cup of the brown liquid sat near Nellie's place. She lifted it to her nose, smelled apples, and took a small sip. It tasted like fire and almost choked her. A couple men who had watched her tittered but kept shoveling food in. "What is this?" she whispered to Charlie.

He took his own sip and licked his lips. "It is hard cider." His mouth twitched, but he managed not to smile. "A Basque drink."

The men talked about the fire and explosion. Most of them worked at the Morning Mine there in Mullan, so had not been exposed to danger, any more than the usual in a mine. Txomin worked at the Gem and commuted every day. He had been out early and patched up to get back to Mullan and the late afternoon *mus* game. Mikel said little during dinner. When the men went back to the card tables, neither Mikel nor Txomin went, staying instead to talk with Charlie. Nell walked out to the automobile to retrieve her camera and set up. She had asked Lorea to turn on all the living room lights, two lamps near the tables, and draw back the heavy curtains on two sets of windows. The room, with its dark-burgundy velvet slipcovers on furniture around the edges, lightened up considerably. Even so, the miners would have to stay still for longer than they otherwise would for any chance of the photograph to be other than a dark blur.

"When I say, 'hold,' can you all keep the position you are in without moving for about sixty seconds—a minute?" The men laughed, and one of them said, "No, then the others will see our signals. We must be secret in our motions, or we will lose our cards."

Nell thought a moment. She wished Charlie were in the room to help her.

Instead, Lorea said, "Do a pretend signal, one you might or might not use, and each of you will not know if it is real or not." She breathed a small sound, one that might have been a laugh. "Or make up a new sign. Help this young lady out."

"You could practice them while I get ready to take your photo. Who knows? This might even make a magazine in Chicago in a story about miners in Idaho." She hoped that sounded enticing to the men. One stood up and retreated to the dining room, clearly uninterested in being shown in a photo.

The others guffawed and jabbed at each other and made stretching motions and tilted their heads right and left and grinned and winked. Even Nellie laughed as she pulled the black cloth over her head, focused her camera, and pulled off the cloth.

"At the count of three, hold your positions, but don't look at me." She slid in the film holder and pulled out the dark slide, counted to three, and opened the lens. She held her breath as she waited to close it again. The men were remarkably quiet and held quite still, looking like a photograph already. "All right. You can breathe again!" Each miner released himself—one or two laughing. Another couple waved their arms. The rest expelled a held breath and joined in the hubbub.

"One more?" Nellie moved her camera and tripod to a different angle. General agreement murmured around the room.

Charlie entered the living room with Mikel and motioned to Nellie that it was time to go. She finished her photo and packed up her gear, thanking the men and Lorea. "Come back anytime for a real Basque meal," she said. "Dominic would like to meet you also. I am sorry he was not here this time."

Back in the auto, Nellie hugged herself. She was full of good food and good spirits from her time with the miners. Charlie said little until they drove away. "We are going to stop at a couple of the 'cafes' and 'soft-drink' parlors on our way out of town, to see if we can get a drink of liquor. Also a cigar store."

"We are? Are you thirsty?" She thought a moment. "You don't smoke cigars."

"No, just doing a little research on our assignment."

"What about the cider we were drinking at dinner? Isn't that illegal?"

"It is, but it was made on Lorea's kitchen stove. We aren't after small entrepreneurs like Lorea and Dominic. We are after the big bootleggers that produce their own liquor from stills, most likely set up along back roads, forgotten mine shafts, or bringing the stuff in from out of state. I am more interested in the poisonous kind, not bonded liquor from Canada, though."

"What about the federal agents? Don't they want each kind of scofflaw?"

"They may want all of them, but there are not enough law enforcement officers in the whole country to make Prohibition stick, especially in the backwaters of states like Idaho and in mining and logging towns like these in North Idaho." Charlie's face carried a grim look, but then he glanced over at Nellie and grinned. "Let us have some fun."

Chapter Three

The first place of business they chose was a soft-drink parlor. The signs in the front window advertised Coca-Cola, ginger ale, fruit juices, and near-beer, whatever that was. A curtain hung from a bar about the middle of the window, so a person walking by could not see into the parlor. At the door, they ran into a man who weaved into Charlie and said " 'Scuse me." Charlie pulled Nell out of the way and waited until the drunk was out on the sidewalk before escorting Nell inside. Chairs and tables sat around in a haphazard pattern with few people sitting. Noise and music came from a back room. They looked at each other. "Shall we enter?" Charlie asked. Nell nodded. "We're here."

Nell placed her arm through Charlie's. He pulled back the curtain for her. A long counter along one side of the room was lined with mostly men, dressed in casual clothes. Several large schooners stood on the counter along with shot glasses and a couple of glasses perhaps filled with grape juice. Two women sidled up to the counter, each dressed in a slinky gown with arms and legs showing as well as cleavage. "Uh-oh." Charlie turned around and escorted Nellie back through the curtain. "Not the place for us," he said.

"Why not? I wanted to see who would be buying 'soft drinks' in a back room." She pulled her hand loose. "Maybe I could take a photograph." She craned her neck to peek through the slit in the curtain. "Or have a glass of . . . of near-beer." She leaned in. "What fun is it to leave before we've even tried to order something?"

A burly man with a shiny pate poked his head through the slit. "Can I get you something, folks? We're friendly 'round here. From out of town?"

The two of them sat on stools in the back room of the soft-drink parlor, and the bartender placed a beer in front of Charlie and a soda in front of Nellie. Perhaps all of this was not a good idea at all.

Maybe Goldie was right. Charlie had wavered about asking Nell Burns to accompany him to North Idaho. He had decided at least to bring up the subject with her and Goldie Bock, her landlady. Goldie was as near to a mother as Nell seemed to have in Ketchum or Hailey, so he may as well broach the subject to both of them.

"I have been asked to visit North Idaho to investigate corruption and the Prohibition law," he had said, once he had them both settled in Goldie's kitchen. That was Goldie's business place, and he wanted her professional acumen, as well as her mothering sensibilities. "Nell's photographic expertise would be useful there. She has dealt with moonshiners in the past, but on an isolated basis. I do not think there is anything dangerous about this assignment, or I wouldn't consider asking you." Charlie tried to keep his voice professional and low. "I thought you both might have an opinion on this request." He leaned against the large kitchen stove.

Goldie straightened up in her chair. Nell studied Charlie with her large, gray-green eyes. A hint of a smile flickered. He wondered what she was thinking—always difficult for him to tell.

"Would you pay her?" Goldie asked.

"Of course. This request comes directly from the federal marshal's office. They are familiar with her photographic work, both from the Stanley Basin and Craters of the Moon. As I recall, she earned a bonus from the photos at Craters, as no one else could have taken them." Charlie hoped he could be forgiven for a small fib. He was the one paying Nellie out of his own office funds, not the marshal's office. He never told the marshal that C. N. Burns was a woman.

The smile finally reached Nell's lips. "Are you thinking I would photograph moonshiner stills and such? Or take photos of illegal whiskey bottles and people drinking?"

Charlie held back an answering smile but straightened himself. He wanted to pace, but the kitchen wasn't that large. "I would think your photographs might be all of those things. I will not know until I get there."

"Speaking of that, how will you get there?" Goldie asked. "There ain't no easy way from south Idaho to north Idaho, is there? Driving it would take days." She didn't add "alone together in a car," but she might as well have.

"The marshal's office will arrange train tickets from Shoshone to Boise to Spokane to Bitterroot," Charlie said. "It is an overnight trip. Separate Pullman berths of course," he hastened to add. He hoped his discomfort from talking about the subject did not show.

"Where will you be staying?" Goldie's face was a series of frowns. It seemed clear she would not approve.

"There is a hotel in Bitterroot, the largest town. There are mines all through the area—lead and silver, mostly. Miners are known for their need for whiskey and beer." Charlie cleared his throat. He was back on familiar ground. He leaned again against the stove. "I am surprised that the Prohibition amendment passed in Idaho, even that Prohibition was adopted in Idaho before it became a federal law."

"And women," Nellie added. "Don't look shocked, Goldie. You know what has gone on in our towns for years. And gambling. I imagine there are 'ladies of the night' and gambling parlors as well as saloons all around the area." She turned to Charlie. "I can just imagine the kind of photographs I could be taking. Would I be allowed to do my own camera work when I wasn't doing yours?"

Goldie interrupted. "Why you? Don't we have enough crime and such here in Blaine County? Let someone else do it." She stood, grabbed a washcloth, and swiped the table where she and Nellie sat.

"Things are quiet around here right now. I do not suppose it will take more than a couple of weeks to obtain the kind of evidence the marshal's office wants." Charlie turned to Nellie. "Of course, you could take all the photos you wanted, maybe even in the mines. As I recall, you did that at the Triumph Mine here and met with success."

"Well, I'm not sure it's proper for Nellie here to go gallivanting across the state alone with you." Goldie tossed the cloth into the sink. "She ain't never listened to me before, so I doubt she'll listen to me now. Besides, if I knew how to take pictures, I'd go with you."

Charlie was glad he didn't have a mouthful of coffee, or he would have spit it out. Instead, he turned to Nellie to see what her response would be.

"You could come with me, Goldie," Nellie said. "You could be our chaperone." Her face clearly reflected her next thought with an eye roll, Not that I would need one.

"I have a business to run here." Goldie shook her apron. "Wish I could, though. Guess I need to keep an eye on Rosy's boys, too." Her face flushed, so she turned her back on her two kitchen guests.

"I guess that is settled, Charlie. I'm coming with you. When do we go? What kind of weather should I expect? I'll need to get extra film and flash materials. Will you take care of reservations at the hotel? I want a room with a view." Nellie stood up as well. "I'll need to visit Twin Falls for supplies."

Charlie realized his mouth was open, so he closed it and then tried to answer all the questions. "Next week. The marshal already arranged for two rooms at the hotel. I do not think there are views in the middle of town, not like here. Maybe Jacob Levine could send the supplies to you from Twin?" He decided it was time to leave before anyone changed her mind.

This conversation passed through Charlie's mind as he watched three miners in the room, or so it appeared, and they were arguing loudly. Their subject was which brothel in town had the prettiest girls. Nellie stood up and confronted them. "I'm a photographer and would like to take portraits of some of the 'ladies of the night.' Where would you recommend I go?"

"Hands down, go to Mimi's in Bitterroot," said one of the grizzled men. The other two nodded their heads.

"Then why are you arguing about the ladies here in Mullan?"

" 'Cause this is where we live, and, besides, the whiskey is cheaper at the houses here," another man chimed in. They all laughed. Nellie joined them.

Charlie decided it was time to go. Nell never ceased to amaze him. He took another sip, even though he didn't even like beer, stood up, took Nellie's arm, and guided her out of the back room. "Did not your mother ever tell you not to talk to strangers?"

"I found out important information for you, didn't I? The brothels sell liquor. That must be a violation of Prohibition." Outside, Nellie placed her hand inside the sheriff's arm again, as if they were a strolling couple visiting the sights of Mullan. "There's a cigar store. Let's go in. You can buy a cigar. It might be handy to give to a miner some time. Maybe a little gift for information."

Charlie laughed out loud. "You sound as if you are from Chicago." He patted her hand and then opened the door to the cigar store, even though it was dark and getting late. A pretty girl manned the counter. "Can I help you, sir?" In the display case were boxes and boxes of cigars. The room smelled of burning cigars, and Nell wrinkled her nose.

"You can help me," Nellie said, pushing her way forward. "I would like a cigar, a good one, for this gentleman here." No other customers stood around, although laughter and music again came from a back room.

Charlie stepped up to the counter, too. "What is going on back there?" He pointed with his free hand.

"Games and soft drinks," the girl said. She leaned forward and winked. "I can bring you a cigar in there, if you like." Then she turned to Nell. "No women allowed."

Nellie lifted her shoulders and shook her hair. "Haven't you heard? We can vote now. If you can take in a cigar, then it seems women are allowed. Besides, where he goes, I go." Nell glanced at Charlie, removed her hand from his arm and marched past him to the door from which the sounds emanated. "Are you coming?"

Charlie followed, feeling a little like a dog on a leash. Nell surprised him on many levels, but this was a new level. He did not think he liked it, but he opened the door and allowed Nell to precede him into a room where men played cards and others stood watching. Several others stood at slot machines, where bells and whistles added to the commotion, as the men's arms pulled on levers and waited for pictures of cherries, apples, and pears to circle and stop. Every single man held a glass or cup.

When the two of them entered, one or two men stared and then more until each face in the room looked at Nellie. All the laughing and noise stopped except for a few *ding-ding-ding*s from the slot machines. Almost without exception, the men wore beards, some full and others stringy. More than one wore a miner's cap, but most were bare headed above flannel shirts and Levis. One man leaned behind a bar with several pitchers of amber liquid. He straightened and looked as if he were going to bark an order to Nell.

"What a wonderful photo all of you would make," Nellie exclaimed. "Could I come back tomorrow night and take one?" She leaned forward, as if conspiring with them. "You can hold soft-drink bottles if you like, but this scene would be perfect for a gentleman's magazine. I'm a photographer, you see."

The man behind the bar seemed to gather his wits. "Out," he said. "Out, out, out." He circled the end of the counter and approached Nell. Charlie rubbed his cheek and waited to see what she would do. Nothing would surprise him at this point. Just then, the front-room girl entered the bar, two cigars in her hand. She wore a short, black skirt and net stockings, below a white, frilled blouse. Perhaps she worked for one of the houses nearby.

"You didn't say which kind you wanted," the woman said to Charlie and sidled up to him, looking at Nell with sly eyes. "The Cuban or the homemade one?" She lifted her hand with one of them. "This one's best, and I can give you a good price." She shifted her gaze quickly to the bartender and back to Charlie. "And a good price on other goods as well." Again, she winked.

Nell swung around and grabbed Charlie's arm. "Clearly, we are not wanted here," she said. "Let's go."

The bartender held the door open for them. As Nell passed him, he said in a low voice, "Come tomorrow and you can take a picture. Will it make me famous?"

"Of course! Especially if you hold a liquor bottle," Nell smiled and said. "But I can't promise anything."

Chapter Four

A knock sounded on Nellie's hotel room door. She moved from the one window, with only a brick wall for a view, to answer it. There stood Charlie, dressed in what looked like mining duds—plaid flannel shirt, Levis, boots, and a canvas jacket. There was no gun visible, nor was he wearing his sheriff's star. That had disappeared before their trip to Mullan.

"We are to go down to the mine accident, Nell. This will be deeper into the mine than we were two days ago. I have permission to bring you and your camera, but it would be better if you wore a hat and pants again. No dresses." Charlie held his Stetson in one hand and drew his other hand through his dark, thick hair.

"So I look like a man or, at any rate, don't look like a woman?" Nellie couldn't resist a pretend scowl.

"Correct. Miners think women bring bad luck in the mines. The less noticeable you are, the better. There was so much pandemonium the other day, I do not think anyone noticed you at all, except when the flash went off."

So much for gallantry, Nell thought, then said, "All right. I'll be down in a jiffy."

The ride in an open-topped man-car into the mine was much the same as her earlier trip. Waiting at the entrance, an electric engine chuffed while men gathered and seated themselves in the flat cars with timber benches and backs on both sides and an aisle down the middle. A few greetings bandied back and forth, but, by and large, the men sat down next to each other and said little. Nell and Sheriff Azgo were heading into the mine with the swing shift. The mountains surrounding the adit climbed steeply, but a weak afternoon sun warmed the riders, until they entered the mine. At first, the darkness absorbed all light but lifted some when the engine's headlight turned on. The smell of damp and dirt felt ordinary, not like the sulfur the day before. The headlight reflected off seeping walls and strings of cables and covered wires. The man-car bumped along for what seemed like a long stretch to reach the main hoist room. Few men were present, a contrast to the day she and Charlie watched the sleds bring up the injured and the dead men. A sense of relief swept through her, until she was instructed about riding down the shaft in one of the sleds—a pickle barrel, their guide Jim said, a shift boss who wasn't on duty the day of the explosion. He was youngish with a black beard and, like the two of them, wore a canvas jacket or "digger," pulled over their clothes, and a tin hat she likened to a helmet.

Jim had several carbide lights with him that he attached to their hats and showed them how to regulate the flame. Little bowls on the lamps held two or three ounces of carbide. Above was a small container with a water control. When the water dripped on the carbide, Jim started it with a flint, and the flame shot out two inches. He tightened the water control so less dripped down. Nellie was certain she did not want to fuss with it and was happy that her guide would do the work. Charlie looked almost as uncomfortable. Neither one of them would make good miners, she thought.

"You won't need the light in the man-sled—only when we get out on Level Thirteen. Keep your head down and your arms inside the car. Otherwise you'll lose one or both." Jim might have been describing walking down a street for all his voice said. Nellie shuddered but said nothing. This was definitely a new experience and not one she might have chosen on her own.

"When we get to the explosion level, we'll get off, and I'll show you around." Jim turned to Nellie. "I understand you want to take photographs. It's much darker there than here." He gestured to the electric lights in the hoist room. "One thing you have to watch out for is, don't touch any wire over your head. It'll fry you." This time, his voice carried an anxious undertone. "We don't want to fry a pretty photographer." His white teeth showed in between his mustache and beard in a quick grin. "One of the superintendents is down there. He was on duty when the explosion happened."

"I'll need someone to hold my flash material if it is dark. Can you do that?" Nellie knew his compliment changed her perspective of the miner. He looked much more handsome than she had first thought, even if she couldn't see much of his face because of the hair. She turned to Charlie. "Or you can, but I suspect you'll want to be prowling around." His hairless face was much more to her liking.

They all climbed into the sled, along with two men wearing what looked like life vests with rubber hoses and face masks dangling in front. Neither had beards. This was a rescue crew, Jim had announced when they showed up. Nellie swung her camera pack over her right shoulder and handed the lighting gear to Charlie to carry. She squeezed her buttocks to get as much purchase on the small wood projections in the man-car as she could, pulled her hands inside, and narrowed her shoulders, keeping one hand on her pack strap. She crowded close to Charlie and wondered what he was thinking about this. She asked him in a low voice, "Have you ever been down in a mine?" He shook his head. Maybe he was as nervous as she was.

The sled sat at about a 45-degree angle on tracks aimed toward a black hole below them. Bells dinged, and the sled began to ease down the track. And then it sped up, faster and faster. Nellie grabbed Charlie's arm.

Jim turned his face towards them from one perch below. "Don't worry. The hoistman knows what he's doing."

They passed three levels where a miner or two were standing, and lights showed a shack or an ore car. In the shaft, huge timbers holding the mountain away from them must have been a foot square. "This is the man-car shaft. The ore gets pulled out in the ore shaft and carried to the mill," Jim said. He droned on in a bored voice. The sled began to slow and stopped at a station, much like the ones they had passed. All five disembarked. Jim gave Nellie a helping hand, but Charlie was already headed toward a pile of wood and metal. Nellie took a huge breath, blew it out, and followed Charlie. She looked above for wires to avoid.

When Charlie introduced Nell to the supervisor, he managed to make her name sound like "Bill." It was all right with her. For all she knew, the man who set off the dynamite was standing right next to her, even if he was a supervisor, or was one of the rescue crew.

"Dad-blamed union members did this," the superintendent said. "They blew up the mill years ago, and now they're trying to shut down the mine." His name was Harry Pierce. Although he had a tin hat on, unlike several of the miners who were bare headed or wore simple knit hats like the one Nellie wore covering up her hair under her tin hat, he had no look of a miner—no beard, no mustache, and his clothes looked freshly laundered. He even wore a suit-type jacket, a dark tweed, as if he would never stoop to mining. His black and bushy eyebrows made up for the lack of a mustache. "I won't have it! I'm callin' in every blasted one of 'em and put 'em in the hot seat." His yell seemed so out of place in the dark, otherwise quiet area.

One of the rescue team said in a low voice, "That'll shut the mine down for sure."

Harry Pierce stabbed a look at the man who spoke, but he calmed down and grunted. "I'll start with the powder monkeys on this level. None of the muckers or timberers could have set up the giant powder to blow like this."

Charlie and the super circled the damage—a metal shed twisted like a pretzel, burned and black as tar. An equally black hole at the edge of the pretzel must have been where the charge went off. Nell followed them as they moved. So did Jim. The rescue team hung out near the shaft. The metal pretzel showed scarred markings, as did more metal pieces in the same stack, as if etched with acid. The men talked in low voices, and the super pointed out one thing or another. She couldn't hear his low growl, so she watched Charlie's face, looking stoic and blank as usual. When his eyes blinked and he made an almost surreptitious movement with his hand, she came forward with her camera.

Nellie set up her tripod, mounted her Premo camera, and walked gingerly toward the ruin, avoiding stepping on anything that wasn't dirt or rocks. She pulled the black cloth over her head and focused. When she uncovered, one of the rescue men stood nearby. "I'll hold the flash material. I've done it before."

With firm hands, Nellie filled the tray and handed it to the man, warning him to be careful and not spill any.

"I know. I know." The tray sagged slightly to the left, and some of the material dropped to the ground. "I got it," the man said. "I got a match. Tell me when you're ready."

She pulled out the slide to expose the film. "Ready!"

The material burst into a white light. Nellie opened the lens and closed it in one swift movement. The men had shocked looks on their faces, the usual response to a flash photo. Nell lifted her tripod and moved toward Charlie. "What else do you want me to take?"

Charlie barely shook his head, but with his hand made a slight gesture to the super. Nellie wondered if he had the same thought she did—that the super or one of the rescue miners could be the culprit. Nellie lifted her tripod and camera and wandered closer to the damaged shack, although it could hardly be considered a shack any more—just a pile of junk. Finally, she found an angle that included the super, Charlie, and one of the rescue men, as well as Jim, their guide. She turned to the rescue man who helped with the flash. "I'd like to take the whole scene."

Rescue Man eyed Nellie briefly, then nodded his head, as if he understood what she was after. He held the flash tray steady while Nellie filled it again. She pointed him to a spot near her side, and he shifted to it, again eying her and then the men, as they continued to poke at the remains of the explosion. He lifted his eyebrows and waited for her signal. A smart man, Nellie decided, asking herself if that was good or bad. Right now, it was good for her.

Again, Nellie set up and focused. She had the sense that Charlie was keeping the other men stationary with his questions, waiting for her as well. Nellie used her hand to signal Rescue Man; he lit the tray, and, once again, the flash burst out like fireworks in a cave. Nellie took the photo and closed her eyes at the same time, to keep her sight when the flash blew. The men all looked up, of course. She watched their expressions. The super was definitely unhappy to be in a photo. The others kept on poking at the scrambled remains. The burnt metal and wood smell still suffused the air around all of them.

"Don't do that again unless you warn us," the super said. "I don't like being shocked like that."

"I'm sorry," Nellie said, not sorry at all. "I wanted a photograph of the whole scene you were all discussing." She began to carry her camera to another angle, not far from the shaft. The other rescue man stumbled toward her, and if she hadn't been watching, he might have hit her camera and knocked it down the shaft, maybe her with it. "Watch out!" Did he do that on purpose or did the super push him from the side not visible to her? Maybe Charlie had seen.

The sheriff moved next to Nellie, as if protecting her. "I'd like another photograph from that far angle. Let me walk you around there. I can hold the tray this time." He took her elbow and shuttled her around the shaft and back towards a drift that angled into the darkness. He motioned for the miners and super to step aside.

Nellie found herself trembling a little as she filled the tray once again. Charlie spoke in a low tone, as if he couldn't actually whisper. "Nice work, Nell." She wanted to ask if he had seen something before he had moved to her side but instead busied herself with the photograph. He held the tray up. "All right, men, another photo. Close your eyes." To Nellie, he said, "Tell me when you're ready, and I'll light the tray."

After they finished with that photograph, Charlie said, "I'd like to walk back on each drift that leads to this station, but I can do it another time." Jim gave a questioning look. The sheriff turned back to Nell. "Why don't we go back up with the super and find out who was on shift that day and where they were. That all right with you, Harry." He didn't add a question mark, as if it were a foregone conclusion that the super would help with names and duties. He nodded to Jim, and they all climbed back into the sled, still waiting for them. Jim yanked the bell to go up. They left the rescue workers behind, and Nell released a held breath.

Chapter Five

Back at the hotel, the front desk clerk handed Nell a note. "This was left for you a while ago. Man wanted to know if you were here and what your room was."

"I hope you didn't tell him!" Nell took the note. This place was certainly not a first-class hotel. The clerk probably gave out her name, room number, and anything else he knew, which couldn't have been much. "Thank you."

She opened the note as she walked to the elevator with Charlie. She saw the signature and a small drawing. "Yippee!"

"What is it?" Charlie asked, holding the elevator door for her.

Inside, Nell grinned broadly. "It is Rosy and Moonshine! I can hardly wait to see them." She flourished the note. "They will wait for us at the Smelter Café and Inn, where they are staying. I had no idea he might bring Moonie." Her spirits soared. After the dark mess in the mine and her fear, even if the stumble against her was an accident, she felt carefree again.

"Does it say how he got here?"

She turned the note to front and back. "No, only that Ross hoped he could find my uncle—does he have a name?—and that he brought his dog to help in the search." Nell smiled. "Guess my telegram worked. But, oh my, does he really want to go back into a mine?" The elevator stopped, and they both exited on the third floor. Their rooms were down the hall from one another, not next door, which was just as well, Nellie thought. She might have been tempted to—what? Her mother would definitely not approve. "Do you want to try and telephone him? Or should we go there? I'm tired and hungry, but I do want to see them, especially Moonshine!"

Charlie walked Nell to the door of her room. "No, I think I should limit my contact with Rosy. If he is a miner supposedly unrelated to what has happened here, we should not be seen together. There is less chance of tying you to my investigation, although . . . ," he said and hesitated. "People are getting to know you around town, I am afraid. More so than they are me. Some of the miners, the people at the hospital, the police . . . You and your camera." He placed his hand over his mouth and studied a spot on the rug. "If he is here to look for your 'uncle,' then it should be all right for you to meet him and even bring him up to your room. You may have to sneak the dog in." His face softened. "I have missed him, too. Even Rosy."

Nell unlocked her room. "I will change into a dress and nice hat and leave my camera in the room. Fewer people know me that way. I'll walk along to the café and inn. Isn't it down across the river? It isn't dark yet, so I should be fine. I'm not sure I want to be strolling the streets, especially those along the soft-drink bars, in the dark. With Moonie here, I would be fine." She waved goodbye and closed the door. She could hardly wait to see her dog.

After a quick bath, Nellie gussied herself up and soon left her room and the hotel. She didn't think to ask Charlie if he had tried to reach Rosy by telephone. The sun had sunk behind the mining mountain, but the light outside was a rich, spring color, fading into a gloaming, a word she loved. She knew it would take her twenty or thirty minutes to walk to the inn where Rosy stayed. She wondered if he had to sneak in the dog, too. There had been no signs about pets at the hotel where she and the sheriff stayed. A dog should be just as welcome as the "ladies of the night," she thought, but maybe not. She passed more than one storefront with the words "soft drinks" and "juice" etched on windows. The signs reading Bar or Saloon had not been removed, but their lights had been turned off. Nevertheless, lights shone onto the street from inside, and occasionally she could hear honky-tonk music and men's voices drifting out open doors. She passed an occasional couple and was ignored. Shops, as few as they were, had closed for the evening. She saw no other women alone and hurried her pace.

At the Smelter Café and Inn—what a dismal name—Nellie stepped into the café. There were customers at the dinner counter and a few in booths around the side. She paused, not certain whether she should go to the inn portion of the establishment. She hated to be asking for a man in that fashion.

And then, she heard a bark from the corner, and a black animal, her black animal, dashed up to her and nuzzled her legs. He stood as high as her knees, and his white teeth shone in what looked like a grin. "Moonshine!" Nell knelt and hugged him. His bark softened to a series of *arp*s. Most of the customers turned to watch with grins on their faces. They all seemed to understand how much love there was between the kneeling woman and the happy dog. Rosy joined them. Nell stood and hugged him, too. He looked his usual grizzled self, but he, too, carried a grin as wide as Moonie's. He sported a black eye patch and a low-slung cap. "My, you are dashing, Rosy! And a sight for sore eyes." She whispered in his ear. "We should get out of the spotlight in the middle of the café."

Rosy took her arm and led her to the back booth where he had been sitting. Moonie followed, and, as soon as Nellie sat down, the dog placed his head on her lap. His dark-brown eyes focused on her own. She looked up. "How did you get here?"

"It ain't easy! I drove my old jalopy. Held up purty well. Moonie liked it, with his head hangin' out the window most of the time. I told him we were goin' to meet you." He grabbed her hand. "It's mighty good to see you, Missy. I hope you've been all right and Charlie ain't exposed you to no criminals here. They's plenty around. I seen one or two already." He nodded his head toward the front of the room where three men, obviously miners coming off shift, jabbered in tones that could be heard all around the café.

None of the faces was familiar to Nell. She heard a reference to moonshiners and Mimi, so she turned her back on them. She did not want to become familiar. "That is a long motor trip. How did Moonie hold up? Will the inn let the dog stay with you here?"

"Sure. Why not? But I plan to get a job and move into a boardinghouse, probably the one up the street from the Gem. Then you may have to take him to your hotel. That's what you want me to do, ain't it?"

"Rosy, we do need your help, but if you don't want to go back into the mine, we will understand. Will the mine hire you with your patch?"

"Don't see why they wouldn't. Mines is always lookin' for powder monkeys, and this one is no exception. I don't plan on stayin' too long. Don't want to leave the boys in Hailey more than a week or so. I'm afraid that ornery sheep man will find out Charlie and I are both gone and he'll kidnap those boys out to the ranch."

"How are Matt and Campbell?" Rosy's two boys had recently arrived back in the Wood River valley from their temporary home with their aunt in Chicago. "I've missed them, too." In fact, Nellie had barely had time to even think about the boys. They were safe in their new home in Hailey and with Rosy's sister. They were both in grade school and were a handful for the aunt. Goldie would be checking on them, too. She thought of springtime in the mountains—wildflowers beginning to peek out, sunshine dappling the bare mountains, fresh clean air. She swallowed a sigh. "How is school going for them?"

"Good. Matt likes it, and Campbell doesn't. He'll get used to it, I guess. I think my sister is getting antsy. She'd rather be back in Chicago. Do you miss it?"

"Chicago? Not a whit. I miss the Wood River valley though. The smelter smoke here is depressing. So is the situation. Are you hungry? I am. Is there a menu? Did you order?"

Rosy handed a grease-stained, multi-page menu to Nell. "I waited for you." He lifted his hand, and a waitress came over with her order book and pencil.

Nell glanced at the menu and ordered soup and beef stew. No lamb on the offerings. Rosy ordered a beefsteak and fried potatoes. When the waitress left, Nell filled Rosy in about the explosion in the mine, the Prohibition law-breakers, and the apparent corruption in two towns up the valley. She didn't know if Bitterroot suffered from the same underhanded violations of Prohibition but suspected that was the case. Charlie would be going back into the mine the next day or so to do more investigating, and she planned to visit the hospital to see what she could learn from the men who were injured. They both hoped Rosy would get on with Gem and see what he could find out from the inside. She also explained about the blacklisting of all union members and warned him not to say anything about a union and deny he was ever in one if asked.

"What about your uncle?" The food had arrived, and Rosy tucked his napkin in his collar.

"I don't really have an uncle here. I did have an uncle, once. He went on the gold rush to the Yukon and was never heard from again. That was to give you an excuse to come up here and do some sleuthing for us." Nell gave Moonshine a piece of her meat. She wondered if a local greengrocer would carry dog food, or if she should save something from all her meals. She had no place to cook any meat she could get from a butcher.

"How is the sheriff doing?" Rosy looked sharply at Nell, as if trying to read her mind.

Nellie could feel herself blush as she smiled. "He is fine. All business, as usual." Then she remembered how he had hugged her to him, and she knew her blush deepened.

"Ha! Looks like more than fine, maybe, and not all business." He glanced under the table. "See that, Moonshine? She might have herself a feller." Rosy's face didn't look all that happy, although he did laugh.

"I'll pay, and you can walk me back home, along with Moonie. We'll sneak both of you into the hotel, and you can see Charlie for yourself. He doesn't want to meet you in public, so you won't be associated with him. He can give you more detail than I have about the goings-on in this town and the others up the road. There certainly are a lot of miners here, and, from what I can tell, many of them live in boardinghouses and don't have families with them. The supervisor who took us down the mine said that quite a few miners move from mine to mine—those in Montana, here, on into Nevada. And he said as soon as hunting begins, dozens take off to shoot deer and elk. Maybe moose and bear, too." Nellie shuddered. "I don't think we will be here that long. At least, I hope not."

The two walked together, and Moonie stayed between them. Rosy gave Nell the leash, but she didn't fasten it to Moonie's collar yet. As they passed the soft-drink establishments, Nell explained that most of the back rooms apparently carried liquor, whether moonshine or smuggled in from Canada, she didn't know. "You might want to stop and meet a few miners. Those in the bars are on the day shift at the mine. The swing shift gets off around midnight, I believe."

Rosy sighed. "All mining towns are alike, I guess. Sounds like Hailey in the heydays, but then there weren't no laws against booze. I'll drink the soft drinks and see what I can find out about where to go to get a job."

"Rosy, do you remember that Three-Fingered Jack, your old friend in Ketchum, was from up here?" That was the first crime Nell became involved with when she arrived in the Wood River valley—an apparently frozen body in a run-down cabin. "You said he played in a band here and in Hailey. Maybe you could ask about him."

"Might work." Rosy rubbed his head. "He was a trumpet player. Damn good one, too."

At the hotel, Nellie, Rosy, and Moonie slipped into the side door and up the back stairs. Nellie knocked on Charlie's door, which he opened immediately and ushered everyone inside. "Glad you made it, Rosy." He shook the miner's hand. "The eye patch looks good on you." He also leaned down and rubbed Moonshine's ears and neck. "Glad to see you too, old boy.

"How are Matt and Campbell?" Charlie stood again and motioned the two of them to two chairs. He sat himself on the bed.

"They're good." Rosy sat down and pulled his hat off. To Nell, he seemed most uncomfortable.

"I filled Rosy in on most everything, but I thought you could give him more details," Nell said. "He is going to stop in one of the saloons on his way back to the Smelter Café and find out about getting a job." She stood and headed for the door. The sheriff slid to his feet.

"You are not going, are you?" He lifted his hand, maybe to stop her, then let it drop.

"Yes, I'm tired. I have some food stashed in my purse that I will give Moonshine. He can sleep in my room. I'll take him for a walk first thing in the morning." She turned to Rosy. "Good night, Ross. I'll have to get used to that name." Nell gave him a quick hug, called Moonie to her, and slipped out the door, amused by the sheriff's expression.

In the morning, Nellie slipped down the stairs with Moonshine. She attached the leash as she stepped out the side door and led her dog to the back of the hotel, where there was an alley of sorts, not paved, and verges of weeds and grass on each side. Up the alley, a large boardinghouse with windows blazing in the dark morning like a multitude of candles greeted her. Miners headed in, and others rushed out, probably to catch the man-cars into the mine for the first shift. She nodded her way past them. A couple smiled at her and Moonshine, and a few more waved, as if they knew her, but she was sure she didn't know any of them. It was hard to tell for certain. Now they would, she thought. A different path would have been a better choice. Down the alley, the lights faded.

Nell realized someone was stepping more rapidly to catch up to her. She looked over her shoulder and saw a tall man in miner's duds. Moonshine growled in the back of his throat, quietly, not yet worried. She kept a tight grip on his leash and moved behind him.

"Wait up, Miss . . ." The miner caught up. "Are you the one taking pictures everywhere?"

"I have taken a few. I'm a photographer, and the mining scenes make extraordinary subjects. Why do you ask?" Moonshine calmed down but stayed alert.

"I thought you might like to visit the rock house and the smelter and take them, too. There's a photographer in Wallace who might buy them from you. He's been down the mine himself, but I don't think there's any pictures of the other workers." He slowed his steps to match hers.

"Yes, I would like to view other workers. I visited a mine in central Idaho, and that photograph was quite successful. How would I go about getting permission to visit the other operations here? All the ore was shipped out down there." She was taken aback that a miner would be interested in her work. "Are you a photographer, too?"

"Me? Hell, no." He covered his mouth. "Sorry, Miss. My name's Julius Weber. I just like photographs. I don't know how to take them."

Nell thought his answer was strange and sounded dishonest. She looked the man over, noting his clean-shaven face, his clean digging jacket, his cowboy boots. She faced him fully. "Are you a miner?"

"No, ma'am. I'm a smelterman. I work in the smelter, not down under. I tried that once and decided it wasn't for me. I didn't want that mountain falling in on me or spilling its guts of rocks over my head."

"Do you live in this boardinghouse?" She gestured back to the well-lit building. This man didn't feel right to Nellie. Maybe she was more used to the hard rock miners, those underground. "I thought only miners stayed there." She wanted to walk away, but he kept pace with her.

"They had an extra room, said I could stay until I found another place. There's another house over by the post office, but only engineers stay there. I'm kinda between a rock and a hard place. Know of anything? You been up the valley taking pictures?"

Now he was getting too chummy. "Sorry, no." Nellie wheeled around, taking Moonie with her. "I hope you find a place." She bit her lip to keep from suggesting the Basque boardinghouse in Mullan. If he hadn't heard of it already, then she wasn't going to enlighten him. "I have to get my dog back and go to work, myself."

"Where are you staying?" He reached out to touch her sleeve.

Nellie pulled her arm away, drew back, and continued to

walk. She pretended not to hear him. He was definitely too snoopy and didn't quite fit the role he assumed. If anything, a smelterman might be even dirtier than the miners. Still, she would like to get inside the smelter. Maybe Charlie could get her in there on some pretense or another. On second thought, she decided not to ask him. He'd think she wasn't keeping her mind on the sleuthing business.

The hospital was on her list to check out and talk with the injured miners. She would have to leave Moonshine in her hotel room for the time being. He might be glad to be off the road and have a warm place to sleep. Before she visited the hospital, she would round up dog food of some kind and a blanket for him to sleep on. She would put a "do not disturb" sign on the door of her room to keep the maids out, not that they had come around. She and Charlie had been in town for four days already, and there were no signs of anyone changing beds or vacuuming floors or dusting. They hadn't moved forward in their investigations of moonshining or murder, either. At the side exit, Nellie already missed Moonshine, her guardian. She lifted her shoulders and strode on toward the hospital. She was not afraid.

Chapter Six

The steps leading up to the front door of the hospital discouraged easy entry. They climbed so steeply, Nellie wondered how a wounded miner could get to the top. There must be an emergency entry, a place where an ambulance or other vehicles could unload damaged goods. The hospital itself stood like an ancient sentinel over the street leading to the mine entrance, not so far for the disabled to go to seek help. Except it wasn't ancient. Its clapboard sides, its several stories, its shiny windows, its roof—all new in 1910 after the big fire, she'd been told, and now painted like a hefty matron calling her children to her for succor—belied the notion of age.

Inside the front door, a wide hallway bustled with nurses and patients and family members. Nellie felt as if she had interrupted a hidden beehive. An open office with a counter to the left carried a sign: All Visitors and Patients Register Here. She stopped at the counter, letting her pack slip to the floor beside her. A woman, not a nurse, greeted her. "What can I do for you?" Her hair was pulled into an iron-colored bun at the back of her head. Silver-rimmed glasses slid from the top of her nose to its bulbous tip.

"I wanted to visit the miners brought in from the mine accident two days ago. I arranged the visit with Dr. Parker. My name is Nell Burns."

"No one can visit those men yet."

"Dr. Parker said—"

"Dr. Parker is not in charge here and had no business saying you could visit. Are you family?"

"No, I'm a . . ." Nell hesitated. Saying she was a photographer didn't seem to be quite the politic profession to be in. It sounded like a newspaper person, a prying profession. She mumbled as she turned her head, hoping to see someone who could intercede for her, but of course she knew no one.

She tried another tack. "I'm with the police department. I have come here to interview the men who can talk about the explosion." She drew herself up as tall as she could, wanting to be at least as tall as the woman in the office—to no avail. "If you'll just tell me where the men are, probably the least injured. I understand your concern, but the police are all concerned, too."

The woman glared at Nell. "The police have already been here."

"I know that. I am doing follow-up work, now that the men have had a couple of days to improve in their condition. Dr. Parker—"

The woman pushed her glasses back up so her eyes stared at Nellie through the glass itself, instead of over the lenses.

"Captain Turner of the police department directed me here," Nell said, changing tactics. "He is short of men at the moment. Do you want me to have him telephone you? What is your name?"

Either the man's name or the request softened the woman's attitude. "Well, of course if Glen Turner gave you permission. That is entirely different. Go to Ward Five on the second floor. Use the stairs and not the elevator. That is for doctors and patients only. The nurse on the ward, Mickey Hettala, will help you." She turned away with a slight *humph* and took a seat at a desk piled high with folders. She didn't look up again, although Nell could feel the woman stare at her back as she walked to a staircase at the end of the hallway, dodging a gurney with a man on it who looked dead and passing by three children and a mother seated on a bench, waiting silently. Their heads swiveled as she walked by.

The stairs climbed to a landing and turned to go up to the second floor. All the halls smelled of the hospital—a cleaner, the acrid odor of ether, furniture polish, stale food like boiled cabbage, and medicine. Ward Five signaled its location by a hallway sign at the top of a closed door with a cloudy glass window. Nell opened it. She was assailed by the smell of burned meat, and she almost gagged. A dozen iron beds, six to one side and six to another, marched across the room in an orderly fashion, and the weak spring sunshine flowed into the room, lending a brightness that neither the first floor nor the upstairs hallway were permitted. The wood floor creaked as she stepped forward. Not a nightingale, she thought.

No nurse seemed to be in the room. Nell studied the beds. All were occupied, but only a few held men who sat up, at least partially if not wholly. The rest held lumps of white sheets and one or two traction devices with legs in casts, but no movement of the bodies. She thought of the poem by T. S. Eliot in a book her mother, a librarian, had sent her: *"Like a patient etherized upon a table."* She approached the nearest bed with a man who looked awake, although his eyes closed from time to time and then opened again.

"Hello," Nell said. "How are you doing? Do you feel like talking?"

The man's head turned to Nellie, and his gaze rested on her for a moment. "Yes, I could do that. What about?" His eyes, as dark as his hair that was wild and wooly looking, closed and then opened again.

Nell thought he might be drugged for pain. "I wondered

about the explosion in the mine. Do you know anything about it?"

Those eyes popped open. "You bet I do. Damned fire burned me and a bunch of the guys in here. I got off easy!" He glanced around the room, moving his arm at the same time. "I was in the back of some of the men, waiting for the sled to come get us. End of shift, finally."

Nell inched closer. "Did you see how it was set off?"

"Couldn't tell for sure. Looked like giant powder exploded in that shed there—and then burst into flames that cut across the sled station—just like there was a fuse waiting for the heat to snake around to us! Dad-blamed criminal is what I say." He grew increasingly agitated, waving his arms around and then trying to get out of the bed. Nell wasn't sure what to do, and then a nurse sidled in next to the bed.

"Now, Tater, no sense in getting upset. You got to stay in this bed another day or two," she said. "I'm sure this nice young woman didn't mean to get you all het up." The nurse glowered at Nellie and motioned for her to back off.

"I certainly did not," Nellie said. "Tater, is it? Where did you get burned?"

The nurse turned to Nellie and stared. "Who are you? What are you doing in here? No one is allowed!"

"Dr. Parker and Chief Turner gave me permission to talk to the men who could talk. I am following up on the police inquiry." Maybe the police chief's name would calm the nurse as it had the receptionist.

"Well, you can't come in and upset these patients. They need rest and sleep." The nurse was about the same size as Nellie, but the starched white hat perched on her dark, curly hair lent an air of authority that Nellie didn't have.

"I'm Nell Burns," she said. "I didn't mean to upset . . . Tater here. He seemed much better than some of the other men, so I approached him first."

"She didn't do nothing," Tater said. "I just got to remember to calm down. Hard to do, with what happened down in the mine." He jerked the sheet closer around his chin. "I got burned on my chest and legs, but not too bad. I got to get back to work soon as I can. Need the money. What else do you need to know, Miss?"

"Do you have any idea who might have set off the dynamite, I mean giant powder, or laid the fuse so men would get hurt? Did you see anyone skulking around?" Nell wasn't even sure what to ask. Probably the police already asked the same questions.

Tater shut his mouth and shook his head. He looked away from Nell. "Can't tell, even if I knew. Someone would get after me and my family. I got to get back to work." He closed his eyes again, and he either slept or pretended to. Nellie closed her eyes for a moment. This was not going to be easy. It hadn't occurred to her that the men might still be afraid.

"Nurse Mickey, is it? I'm Nellie Burns. Is there anyone else I could speak with and perhaps take a photo? We are trying to find out who caused this devastation." Nell gestured with her arm around the room. She could hardly stand the burnt smell but wanted to carry out her plan to talk to some of the injured. The police may have already, but Nellie suspected she could get further than they had, which was nowhere so far.

The nurse glanced around the room. "No one here. They are in too bad of shape." She turned and gestured for Nellie to follow her. "Come with me. One of the men is ready to go home. I have him in a side room, so he could get dressed and wait for Dr. Parker to come and discharge him." Nurse Mickey led Nellie out the door of the ward and neared a door close by, also one with clouded glass in it. She knocked. "Ira, are you decent? I want to come in."

A muffled voice answered. "Yep. Don't mind my bare legs though." A soft laugh followed.

Nellie looked at the nurse. She smiled and said, "Ira likes to joke." She opened the door slowly and peeked around it, then opened it wider for Nellie to enter, too. "Here's a pretty lady to talk to you. Leave your pants on, Ira," she added as he made a motion to unfasten a pair of Levis. "She isn't interested in your bare legs, just your head."

"Goldarn. I been waitin' for someone to show 'em off to." He turned to look at Nellie and then gave a long, low whistle. "Wowee! I got good lookin' legs. Sure you don't want to see 'em?" His voice was soft with a southern tinge to it.

Nellie felt herself blush. She was glad he was in fact dressed and wasn't sure how to respond, so she glanced at Nurse Mickey. "Nurse, maybe I should wait outside? Does the doctor need to—"

"No, Ira's just joshing." She turned back to the patient. "Sit down, Ira. This lady is here to ask you some questions about the fire in the mine. She's from the police."

"Ha, best lookin' copper I've ever seen." He sat down on the side of the bed in the room. His whiskers looked as if they had been recently shaved and not well. Both the pieces of whisker left on his face and the hair on his head were pepper and salt, only his hair was as curly and thick as a sheep's. His cheeks were ruddy and his blue eyes, piercing. The smile wrinkles around his mouth and eyes softened his appearance from what otherwise might have resembled a hawk. "OK, Mickey, leave us alone. I got some information to get off my chest—and it ain't my shirt." He plucked his own sleeve with a heavily bandaged hand. "And I can't do my boots. Maybe she can help me."

"Ira, she is not here to string up your boots. I'll take care of that. I'll leave you alone for fifteen minutes. Then I'll get the doc in here to let you go. Be nice to her. Her name is Nellie

Burns." She opened the door and slipped out.

The man's face sobered up, and he motioned Nellie to sit down in the chair beside the bed. "I haven't told anyone else about this, but you clearly ain't from this town, as our chief wouldn't hire no girl, so it oughta be safe. But you can't tell anyone at the police station here. If there's an honest cop in this town, I ain't found him. They're all paid by the mining company or the bootleggers." He moved to lean his back against the iron bedstead and lifted his legs to rest on the bed cover. His socks looked gray from washing and darning. Nellie wondered if he did his own darning, it was so rough looking.

So far, Nellie hadn't said two words. If she wanted information, she needed to speak up and, she sensed, be straightforward with this man. "I am with an out-of-town sheriff. He is trusted by the federal marshal for the area, and I trust him, too. I'm his photographer. I will tell him whatever you tell me, but he won't pass it on unless you give him permission to do so." She hoped she was right on that count.

"I was on the incoming pickle barrel, up at the top. The sled always slows down as it comes in for a landing, so I seen what happened. That shack popped up into the air like a jack-in-the-box, and fire spread around the shaft and across it, almost like a river. Then it climbed up the barrel I was in. Just before that, I seen a man sneaking off down the drift behind the shack. I didn't remember that until after I woke up from whatever the doc gave me—ether or somethin' in that cuttin' up room." He lifted his bandaged hand. "Got tore up pretty bad." He smoothed his pant leg with his other hand, brown and strong looking with long fingers and hair on the back.

"Do you know who the man was? A name? A description?"

Ira shook his head. "There was somethin' familiar about him, but, so far, I haven't pegged it." He clamped his lips together and frowned. "I'll keep thinkin' on it."

"Did you have any sense whether it was a company man or a union man? The company seems to think the union had something to do with the explosion."

"There ain't many union men left in here 'cause the company won't hire 'em. They're all on a black list. I ain't pointin' out any union man, because they'd be fired without so much as a 'by your leave.' "

"Half a dozen men were killed. Did you know any of them?"

"I don't have all the news about who was kilt and who wasn't, except the men in Ward Five." He pointed the thumb on his good hand to the wall. "There's somethin' else, though. When I got off shift the night before, I was late and had to call up the sled to come get me. No one else around, but, when the sled come to a stop, I heard someone down the drift where I'd come from. I called out sayin' to hurry up to catch the sled, but no one answered or showed up, so I went up by myself. I couldn't understand that because I'd checked the board, and everyone else had checked out, 'cept me."

There was a knock on the door, and Nurse Mickey opened it again. "Doc is here. You want to go home or not?"

Ira was all smiles again. "Sure do. Get me outta this blood and gore setup!" He moved his legs around so he was sitting up straight again. He lifted his arm as a doctor came in. "Thanks, Doc. You sure fixed me up. Think I'll ever mine again?"

Dr. Parker stood as tall as Sheriff Azgo, although he was much older and hunched forward slightly. His hair was all gray and his face lined, maybe from worry as much as age. He had no laugh wrinkles like the two miners Nellie had talked with. His face was as pale as theirs—apparently none of them spent much time in the sun, although Ira's unbandaged hand was brown as a coffee bean.

"You'll be fine in a few weeks. But, in the meantime, don't

use that hand—no lifting, no hitting. Are you right or left handed?"

"A little bit of both, ambi—, amdib—"

"Ambidextrous? Do you play baseball?" Nellie asked.

"Yes, I do, Miss. I can pitch with either hand. And the season will be getting goin' here pretty soon. I'll use my right hand. It works better anyway." Ira looked about to stand up, but the doctor stayed him with a hand on his chest.

"No mining for the time being, unless you can get yourself a one-handed job."

"Wal, Doc, what'm I goin' to use for money? I got a little saved up, but it'll not last long. You got a job for me here at the horse-pistol?"

"I'll check with the mine office. There might be something you can do, but maybe not underground. The union has a disability fund, you know."

"I ain't no union man," Ira protested. "You want to get me fired?"

The doctor shook his head. "Even so, I'll give you a note. You can use it however you think best." He patted Ira on the shoulder and turned to Nell. "Are you getting any information you can use?"

"Not much. The men are still too damaged." She avoided looking at Ira but then turned to him. "Is it all right if I take a photo of you, Ira? And with your hand up?" She took in both men. "Maybe the doctor could stand next to you? You're both such handsome men!"

"You don't need me, Miss Burns. Good luck with your project." Doc waved at both of them and left the room.

Ira laughed. "I ain't handsome, but I'd like a photo to send to my mother, so sure." He adjusted himself so he stood by the bed. "My hand might worry her, though."

"I'll take two." Nellie moved back to set up her camera and

take advantage of the light coming in the window. "And then I'll tie your shoes." When she finished, she leaned down, tied Ira's shoes, and then took his address, so she could take a photograph to him. So far, she hadn't found a studio where she could develop her film, but she had noticed a photography storefront along the street heading to the mine entrance, farther uptown. "I am staying at the Callahan Hotel, Ira. If you think of anything else you saw, would you telephone me there or send a message? I can come visit you at your boardinghouse."

Nellie opened the door for him as the nurse hurried up. "Off you go, Ira. You can pick up the pills the doctor prescribed uptown at the drugstore. Only take what you need for pain."

Ira frowned. "Do you think I'm a sissy?"

"No, you're not. But your hand may begin to hurt after a while. It will heal faster if you deaden the pain. Come back in two days to get the bandage changed."

"Right-o, Nurse Mickey." And he scooted off.

"Do you want to talk to anyone else, Miss Burns?"

"So far, I am not making much headway," Nellie said. "Have you heard any of the men talking about the explosion? Do they say anything in their sleep?"

"Mostly, they moan and groan, or are unconscious. Ira probably told you that naming anyone could cause a problem, what with the blacklist and all with the union." She leaned close to Nellie and kept her voice low. She looked up and down the hallway, empty for the moment. "I could meet you after work, if you like. I think I do have some information you and that out-of-town sheriff could use."

Nellie wondered if Nurse Mickey had been listening from the other side of the door while Nellie talked with Ira. Either that, or word got around in such a close-knit community. "Yes, we both will be at the hotel. You could talk to either of us. I do have to find a photograph studio. Do you know of one?"

The nurse gestured towards uptown. "A young man just opened one up the street. The Hope Studio. You might stop in there. Tell him what you told us—you're doing some work for the police, but do emphasize you are from out of town. He might not want to help a competitor, although he is as nice as can be." The nurse blushed at her last words.

"Thank you. See you later at the hotel?" They nodded at each other, and Nellie left to take the stairs down. She felt as if she had made some progress. She wondered how Charlie had done with the miners coming off shift. Would they even talk to him?

Chapter Seven

Sheriff Charlie Azgo hated the ride down into the mine as much as Nellie said she did, but he felt that he had no choice, and he did not want to talk about it. All these men worked in the mines, day after day, week after week, and year after year. He feared they would laugh at him if he expressed his trepidation. Even the Basque miners he knew or had met at the Mullan boardinghouse treated the descent into the mines as nothing more than a usual ride to work. He never thought he would miss being a sheepherder in the Idaho mountains around Ketchum and Hailey, but he definitely missed the freedom of the outdoors. The claustrophobia he had experienced in the caves at Craters of the Moon, which he had also felt compelled to hide, was small potatoes compared to the suffocating sense and heavy burden of the mountain above him here in the Gem mine. He smiled at himself over the idiom. He was truly an Idahoan.

Nevertheless, he wanted to meet the miners on their own ground—not at the end of the day outside when they would be hurrying off to a meal at home, to their boardinghouses, to entertainment, either in bars or brothels, for which the north Idaho towns were known. Dozens of miners milled in the deep shadowed area back from the man-car station on Level Fourteen, where the shaft yawned open to even lower levels. Harry Pierce had suggested one of the more active drifts in the mine for Charlie to begin his quest to find out about the explosion at Level Thirteen. He had checked with the Croat miner he met at the café next to the hotel, Izzie. That man questioned his senses when Charlie said he wanted to go down the mine.

Charlie side-stepped away from the edge of the shaft and joined a knot of miners who stood together, also off to one side, apparently not in a hurry to catch the next man-car as it slid down into view. "I am new here," he said. "I heard there was an explosion the other day. Should I be worried?" He wasn't concerned about his slight accent; many of the men came from other places, other countries even.

One of the shorter men, his face sagging with what looked like perpetual tiredness, said, "Are you one of those Pinkerton men? If so, scram." A couple others nodded.

"Do I look like a Pinkerton? I am a Basque. Txomin told me I could get a job here, and I did. But I am used to the outdoors, sheep herding in south Idaho." He scratched his face. "I am used to rattlesnakes, wolves, and coyotes—not dynamite." He tried to slouch like some of the other men. "My name is Carlos."

Another man spat. "A spic."

Charlie shrugged his shoulders. "If you say so. Basque are a race older than the Spanish, than the Mexicans. Than even you, Whitey." The sled took a group of men up the shaft, and Charlie wished he were with them. He could feel the sweat breaking out on his neck and back.

The other men laughed. The short one who spoke first, said, "I'm Mike—over from Butte." He put out his hand, and Charlie took it. The man tried to squeeze the bones in his hand, but he was no match for Charlie's strength. He let go. "Guess you're no Pinkerton. They're all pansies." He pulled himself up. "I'm a powder monkey myself. Dynamite. The main thing to watch out for are rock bursts when you're drilling. That explosion on Level Thirteen was set off by someone—no accident. And it wasn't no union man." He looked around at his group, all of whom nodded. "What's your job?"

"I am not drilling. I am shoveling ore—a mucker." Charlie hoped he had the right terminology. Izzie had schooled him. "I am meeting a foreman who will show me the ropes down here." He gestured back down the drift behind the group. "Swing shift." He knew he would have to wait for the last sled up and wondered if he could last. "Who would set off an explosion on purpose? This work is dangerous enough already, is it not?"

"Good question," one of the others answered. "Probably a super wanting to get rid of the union, so the union was blamed."

More nods. Charlie said, "They asked me if I was union. I said no. That is what Txomin told me to say. Who cares?"

"The owners care. Ever since the revolt back in '99. All the men who worked then and anyone else who belongs to a union in Butte or wherever are blacklisted. No jobs. Keep telling them you ain't a union member. But if you want to join up, come to the Miners' Hall down by the railroad station. The only way to fight the owners for decent wages is through the union." The speaker stopped talking as several more men joined the group.

"You talkin' union again, Mike? They're all Bolshies. That's why they're not allowed in here." The man looked suspiciously clean, as if he didn't work in the mine at all.

"Not me," Mike said. "I drill the holes, stuff the giant powder, and get out." He turned away and led several of the men close to where the sled would return. "Time to get out." He gave a short laugh and nodded at Charlie. "Remember what I told ya."

Charlie wandered away from the new group and found himself beside a miner who looked him up and down and turned away. His beard was black as Charlie's would be if he grew one. "Just coming on shift," Charlie said. "I am supposed to meet a man named Buddy Rinaldi. Know him?"

The two groups of men Charlie had left began shoving each other. The sled slowed into sight and stopped. A man in a canvas jacket jumped off with a nimble leap. "Hear, hear. Stop that, you muckers! Get on out. No fighting down here. Take it to the boxing ring. You all know that!" He pulled at one of the men who had talked with Charlie and aimed him to the sled. "Go on now, or I'll pull every one of you off the shift."

"That's Buddy Rinaldi," the miner told Charlie. He leaned closer. "Don't talk union with him, or you won't last a day. Otherwise, he's an all right man. Not like some of the others." He left Charlie to line up for the sled, then turned his head and added, "Watch him, though. He has a temper."

The shift leader looked past the lineup and aimed his way toward Charlie. "I'm Buddy Rinaldi. You can call me Mr. Rinaldi." He grinned and put out his hand, clean and strong in Charlie's grip.

"I am Charlie Azgo. My Basque name is unpronounceable, so Charlie will do. Do you know what I need?"

"Super Pierce said you wanted to check out the drifts leading to the explosion, but first to get an idea of the workings. This level is good for that, and then we can go up to Level Thirteen to the damaged hoist station. I understand you've been there already. See anything?"

"Other than the twisted metal and fire marks, not that I could tell. I had a photographer take pictures so I can study the damage when I get them blown up and back." He fussed with the light on his tin hat, not remembering how it worked.

Rinaldi showed him how to drip the water onto the carbide to get a steady light. Charlie needed refreshing, so he said nothing.

"Show me the photos, and I can help you identify stuff, maybe," Rinaldi said. Then the two of them headed down a tunnel, dark and slightly oozing under foot. To Charlie, it felt like a wormhole. The sound was a *squish splat, squish splat* for each step they took. They stayed to the side of narrow rails. The farther from the station they moved, the darker it grew. Charlie shrugged his shoulders to release some of the tension he could feel growing in himself. There was a notch in the drift where Rinaldi stopped.

"We'll go down these ladders, the raise, to get into a stope, so you can see how the miners and muckers work. This one'll be empty because of the shift change, but muckers will be showing up soon to shovel the ore down to the next level." He swung his body over the hole and began stepping down a wooden ladder. He had a paunch, but he moved quickly.

Going down ladders in the dark was not something Charlie wanted to do, but he had no choice. He had asked for the tour. He had thought the two of them would walk along the tunnels and come across men drilling and shoveling, shoveling and drilling. He eased onto the upper end of the ladder and could see Rinaldi's light below him, steadily getting smaller. Charlie placed his boot on one step and lowered himself to reach the next one, which cracked lightly as he stepped down.

"Some of these steps are in bad shape," Rinaldi called up, his voice almost buried in depth. "Might want to test 'em as you move down. Or use the sides."

"How many ladders are there?" Charlie asked back.

"Ten, twelve maybe. We'll be heading down about eighty to a hundred feet."

Charlie gripped the ladder sides—also wood—in case a step broke. He didn't want to fall down eight stories of ladders, although he supposed he would land on Rinaldi first. Still, the raise wasn't all that big around. He had begun to think there was no end to the steps down when he realized Rinaldi no longer moved down but stayed in one place. Charlie's boot hit the ground, and he eased himself toward the man.

"Where is the dynamite set? And do the men carry it around with them?" Charlie realized some of his questions might be dumb ones, but Rinaldi didn't seem to care. In fact, he talked like he might be teaching a class in mining, something he seemed to like.

"This here is a stope, where the mining takes place. Watch the piles of ore around. The last shift set giant powder and blew it after they got to the top. The muckers'll come and shovel all of it down that ore chute over there." He pointed to yet another hole in the ground. "It'll go down to the next level where the chute door is closed. Then a skip tender'll come along and open the doors to load the ore into cars. One of the more dangerous jobs down here because sometimes the rocks and muck get jammed and won't move without help from some dynamite. The cars go to a big ore shaft where the ore'll get loaded and taken to Level Nine to go out to the grid in the rock house, then to the separator, and finally the smelter. All in all, it's an impressive operation."

Rinaldi guided the two of them over a couple of ore piles to the end wall. He jabbed with his index finger in a circular pattern. "The powder monkey drills holes around this wall and tamps in the giant powder, the dynamite. He sets clamps with nitro and fuses. Another miner uses an instrument like a long stick with a flat end to scale down the sides and overhead to get extra rock before it falls down. Then the men climb up the raise, and the monkey sets off the fuses. He shouts 'fire in the hole' to warn others, and they quick-step down the drift up above. A swing shift mucker, the shift you'd be on as a new man, moves rocks from the day shift to the ore shaft. Once it's near clean, the timberers put in a square set, like these." He walked over to the timber set up like a house frame and laid his hand on one. "That keeps the headwall from cavin' in."

Charlie studied the area, looking up, down, and sideways. "Does all the dynamite go at once?"

"No, it goes in a pattern, with the bottom row last to push all the material out and into the room for the muckers to deal with."

"How does the miner know how much dynamite to use?"

"Kind of depends on his experience. He'll work the same stope for days, maybe weeks, on end. Before he gets down to his stope, he stops and orders up the powder in a dynamite room along the drift. There's usually twenty to thirty-five or more holes to be drilled and tamped."

"Can I see that room?"

"Sure. Detonators and fuses are there, too. The nipper will bring the giant powder, detonators, and fuses on a track cart, along with a scaler and the drill if needed. Then the miners will lower all of it down the raise with a pulley and rope. The drill is the heavy piece. Sometimes, the miner will leave it in the stope as far back as possible, once the diggings have moved away from the man-way. You can see one back here," he said and pointed. "Drilling is damned dirty work. Gem is trying out some hydraulics in a coupla stopes near Level Nine—a drill that spurts water to cut down the silica dust. Should cut down miners' con too—silica in the lungs. Consumption. Old-timers end up with pneumonia or worse. All the beards you see? Supposed to catch the dust. 'Course, there's still rock bursts." Rinaldi stretched his head around, his eyes white as he seemed to search for weaknesses in the walls.

"What's a rock burst?" The term sounded lethal.

"Where the rock cracks or bursts and kind of explodes. You never can tell when or where it might happen. It's called an air blast, too. Some miners can sense one about to break, and they'll clear out, dragging their workmates with them. Other times, a whole ceiling or headwall will split open and bury the miners. Other times, it's just like a mini-earthquake." Rinaldi shook his head. "Mostly, you can't tell. Nearly all the mine accidents come from rock bursts or timbers busting." Rinaldi and Charlie had stepped back to the ladders, the raise.

"What happens when all the lead or silver is mined out of a stope? Seems like the mountain would become a Swiss cheese chunk. Is that why the rock bursts?" Charlie asked.

"Good question. Besides trying out hydraulic drills, the Gem is moving waste rock and sand back into some of the mined out areas. They think it might help. It's all fairly new." Rinaldi placed his foot on the ladder. "It's all hard work." He began his climb. "You should talk to Gordon Benuti. He suffered a burst, and now he's crippled and in a wheelchair." He swung up.

Charlie took a last look around, eying the rocks, studying the timbers, wondering if anything would break or crack right down on him. He hurried up the ladder behind Rinaldi, much faster than when he came down.

At the top, the shifter led the way to the explosives room. He used a key to open it. Long yellow strings of fuse hung in coils on the wall. Boxes stacked along the walls held the dynamite in sticks. "You used a key," Charlie noted. "Is the dynamite room not open to anyone?"

The man shrugged. "First lead opens it in the morning so the powder monkeys and nippers can get at it. After all the rounds go off in the afternoon, a lead'll come and lock up again."

"Always?"

"Pretty much, I'd say." Rinaldi turned to look Charlie square in the eyes. "You think someone stole giant powder, don't you? Maybe a lead?"

"Just speculating, Mr. Rinaldi. What if a, um, powder monkey doesn't need all the dynamite he asks the—the nipper?—to bring to the stope? Does that ever happen?"

"I'm sure it does. And sometimes, a miner'll want more sticks and send the mucker up to get them. Either way, the dynamite could come out of the stock on any of the levels." Rinaldi picked up a small vial and handed it to Charlie. "These are ammonia nitrate and fuel oil. If you squeeze, you'll get your hands all oily. They vaporize when they explode. That makes gas, and the gas expands and breaks the rock.

"These here are detonator cords," Rinaldi added, pointing to lengths of yellow cord, "used to initiate the caps." He repeated his explanation about drilling holes. "The center hole detonates first and then 'boom, boom, boom' as the others explode." He swept his arm around. "Say, you ask a lot of questions. Did Harry Pierce put you up to it?"

Charlie ignored the question and tried to absorb the information, and then looked into one of the open boxes. "This is the giant powder," he said. There were stacks of silvery gel sticks wrapped in paper. He picked one up. It was over an inch thick, a little over a foot long, and heavy. "If the miner takes the fuses up the ladders, how does he set them off and not burn the ladders?"

"The old-fashioned way, with matches. He props the fuses against the dirt side of the raise, the man-way. They lead to the detonators at the bottom of the hole. The detonators set off the caps, and the caps set off the dynamite."

Charlie nodded. It would take a miner with experience, he thought, to set up the explosion at the shaft station and time it to get men heading off shift. Someone must have been waiting to detonate at just the right time. He glanced around at Rinaldi and found the man staring at him.

"A powder monkey is a miner with experience with explosives. They get paid more 'cause they're worth more than the run-of-the-mill mucker." Rinaldi didn't add "like you," but he implied it.

"How about a shift lead, like you?" Charlie tried not to infer that Rinaldi might have set off the explosion, but the implication hung in the air.

Rinaldi laughed, a sharp, staccato sound. "Ha ha. I'm one of the few leads who could actually do it," he said. "I didn't, but most leads don't have explosives experience. They got their positions by brown-nosing the supers." He gestured for Charlie to exit the room. "I got to be lead because I know what I'm doing." His face frowned. "Probably why I'm taking care of you." To Charlie, he sounded angry but said nothing more when he stopped briefly and leaned over the detonator box. Charlie was surprised to see him take a handful of detonators but said nothing. The shifter closed the door and locked it again. "Let's head up to Level Thirteen so we can both look at the damage and check out the drifts there. I'll deliver these detonators to a miner who asked for them." He shoved them into his pocket.

The two walked back to the hoist station and waited. Rinaldi rang the bells, and Charlie tried to remember the order: two dings, pause, then five dings in quick succession. After ten or fifteen minutes, the sled appeared from below, and they climbed in. Rinaldi rang the bell again—four fast dings. "Where did the"—Charlie slapped the inside of the sled—"come from?"

"Pickle barrel." Rinaldi grinned. "Probably dropping off shifters at lower levels." He looked at his watch. "They should mostly be in place, or will be, including the stope we just left."

On Level Thirteen Rinaldi and Charlie circled the mess. The sled was able to drop off and pick up men, so Charlie had asked the super to leave the stack of twisted metal for a few more days, until the Pinkerton man got there to begin his investigation. Drifts, inside tunnels without an exit to the air, led off in two different directions, not quite opposite each other. The two of them pushed their lights higher and walked down one leading off to the right of the station. Charlie wasn't sure what to look for, but Rinaldi said there should be some evidence of a burned fuse. They found nothing. When they aimed for the other drift, Charlie noted it was almost to the left of the shaft, the side away from where most of the men had been hurt, according to the super's description of the explosion and the aftermath.

Charlie crouched along the sidewall and pointed. "Is this what we are looking for?" Gray ashes like a long worm split in pieces along the edge, and appeared and disappeared. Rinaldi joined him.

"Yup. That is what I would expect from a burned fuse leading to a stash of dynamite." In the dim light from their headlamps, Rinaldi's face reflected a series of downward wrinkles from his forehead to his chin. "Damn. Clear this was no accident."

"Did you think it was?"

"Guess I hoped so. Hate to think one of our miners, or anyone else, would deliberately kill men in this mine. Let me get a flashlight, and we'll see how far this extended." He shook his head. "Accidents happen, but sabotage?"

Chapter Eight

Nellie inhaled the air outside the hospital in big gulps. Even though her nose and throat were getting used to the smelter smoke, she continued to feel the slight burn. She was glad to leave the clinical smell behind her and in particular the singed skin odor that had not left her nostrils after leaving Ward Five. She wondered if the doctor and nurses ever left that odor behind.

In spite of the smoke, not really discernible to the eye during the day, a spring air flowed from the unfurling leaves on the maple trees, the first green blades of grass along the sidewalk where she strode uptown, and a few early crocus and daffodils. The flowers surprised her. The hills rising up immediately behind the businesses along McKinley Avenue maintained their late winter brown and gray, relieved only by the few evergreens still on the slopes. Stumps and slash from logging operations reminded Nellie of a dog's hide with mange. Just thinking about a dog brought Moonshine to mind. She missed him, and, now that he was here, she wanted to get back to her room. The mine office was down the street in the opposite direction she was heading. She wondered if Rosy had been successful in getting a job.

As she approached the uptown area, she decided to stop at the Hope Studio to inquire about developing the film she had already exposed. Not many photographers would be as helpful as Jacob Levine in Twin Falls had been to her, both before and during her sojourn as a crime photographer. Maybe the police facilities included a darkroom, but she doubted it. Besides, if the police or town fathers were involved in the moonshine business or, worse, the mine explosion, she wanted her photos to be available only to Charlie and herself—at least initially.

A bell tinkled as Nell stepped inside the narrow storefront with the calligraphic sign Hope Studio in gold on the door. A counter stretched across the interior, with a space to go behind it at one end and a gauze curtain acting as a wall to what Nellie hoped were a studio and a darkroom. Colorized photographs of brides, couples, and babies decorated the side walls. Even as the door closed, a man swept aside the curtain to greet her.

"You must be C. N. Burns, crime photographer, accompanying Sheriff Asteguigoiri from Ketchum, Idaho." He reached his hand out, and Nell gripped it so she wouldn't be accused of a limp handshake.

"Yes, I am. But how do you know?"

"I'm Walter Hope. I always make it my business to know the competition." The man stood a few inches taller than Nell, with sandy hair and hazel eyes. He was clean-shaven, and his smile lit up a face that otherwise seemed bland and unremarkable, especially after the definitely individual faces of the miners and the patients in the hospital.

Nellie smiled in return. "I am not really your competition," she said. "I am only in town for a specific purpose. Once that is accomplished, we will return to Ketchum. I wonder if I could use your darkroom to develop and print my exposed film. I am sure the sheriff could arrange some compensation for the use of your supplies and for the time I tied up your facilities." She didn't want to mention the moonshiners or the mine explosion, but if Mr. Hope already knew about her, he probably knew what the sheriff and she were investigating. He might even have an opinion or knowledge that could help them. "Nurse Mickey

Hattala said you might be willing to help." At the nurse's name, the photographer blushed in almost the same shade the nurse had—a slight pink tone on otherwise pale skin. Clearly, he did not get outside very much, nor did the nurse.

"Ah, I could arrange that," Mr. Hope said. "I have plenty of developer and fixer. If I get low, the Barnard studio in Wallace probably has sufficient supplies. I can also order in from Spokane, but it takes a day or two to get them here. Are you in a hurry?"

Always, Nell thought. "The sooner the better, I suppose. I don't want to inconvenience you." She gestured to the photographs hanging on the walls. "You must have a busy clientele."

The pink tone almost changed to red. "Ah, some of those photos come from my previous studio in Missoula. I wanted to move further West, find new opportunities and, who knows, maybe find some gold, too." He uttered a short laugh, as if he were joking, but Nell took him at his word. She wondered if he went out panning for gold on his days off. The sheriff told her that many men did explore the canyons and streams outside the valley and lay claim to plots here and there. The result was often skirmishes with moonshiners who also set up their stills in the backwoods—gold of another sort since Prohibition began. He thought the 'shiners made more money than the gold seekers. The deep mines looked for and found silver and lead veins in the ground. Few of the corporate establishments sought gold, as mostly it was found in rivers, showing up as gold dust or small nuggets. The gold strikes attracted the gold rushers, but they, too, moved on when their prospects diminished.

Nell almost missed Mr. Hope's offer of the darkroom as she speculated. "Now? Right now?"

"I am out of the darkroom for the rest of the day. Do you need to go somewhere to get your undeveloped film?"

"No, I carry my film box in my pack." Nell slipped her pack

off her shoulder. "Yes, I could work for an hour or so, if you're sure that would be convenient, and you have sufficient supplies." She was hungry and wanted to share her information from the hospital with Charlie, but both needs could wait. She knew he especially wanted the photos from inside the mine. "I don't have paper or any supplies with me," she began.

"Ah, the sheriff came by and talked to me about doing work for you both," Mr. Hope said, laughing. "That is how I know your name and his."

"You are one of the few people who can pronounce his name. In Ketchum and Hailey, we all call him Sheriff Azgo." She picked up the strap on her pack. "All right. Lead me to your darkroom, Mr. Hope. And thank you!"

The studio owner led Nell back behind the curtain and to a small, neatly organized darkroom, smaller than Jacob's in Twin Falls, but well supplied. He pointed out various aspects of the room including the sinks, the pans for developer and fixer, where to hang the negatives to dry, and the location of the supplies and paper she needed. He left her to go to work. Soon, she hummed as she worked and developed all the negatives from inside the mine. As the negatives dried, she studied them closely—seeing them in reverse, white images on black background. She had noted 8x10 print paper, twice the negative size, which was 4x5. She extracted several sheets for prints from each negative when it dried. Using what Nell thought was a fairly up-to-date enlarger, she would be able to print the photos of the damaged shift shack, too. She would wait to print the photos of the men in the sled as they were brought up from below to the main hoist level. Charlie could look through these negatives and decide if he needed them or not.

Nell checked her watch—almost 5:00. No wonder she was hungry and her back ached. She also remembered her meeting with Mickey, the nurse. She packed up her film box, used a handy envelope for prints, and left the darkroom. Mr. Hope was not around, so she exited the back area and found him in front with Mickey. Their heads were close together across the counter, as if they were telling secrets to each other. Or something else.

As she came through the curtain, they moved apart, the pink tones blushing their fair skins again. "Thank you so much, Mr. Hope. Hello, Mickey. Maybe we could walk together up to the hotel?" She busied herself with her pack, so they could recover from her surprise entrance.

"Oh, yes, yes." Mickey still blushed. "That would be fine. Thank you, Miss Burns." She gathered her purse and gloves but still seemed at cross purposes. "Goodbye—Mr. Hope."

Nell stepped outside the studio where the afternoon sun was dropping lower, almost to the mountain tops on the west side of town. Truly, the valley was deep and the mountains high enough, although not jagged like the Rockies, to give sun a limited time to shine and warm up the mining town. Maybe by May or June, it would feel more like spring than a pinched end to winter. There was snow on the shady side of buildings and definitely in the gulches leading north and south. She shivered, wishing she had donned a warmer outfit. The darkroom had been warm and cozy.

Mickey closed the door behind her as she met Nellie. "I—we—"

"—are stepping out together?" Nellie put a smile in her voice. Momentarily, she felt like an elderly aunt to the young nurse. Nonsense, she thought. She was not that much older than Mickey. Maybe the last year or so had aged her, dealing with murders and mayhem, and frustrated by her own lack of progress in "stepping out" with the sheriff or Jacob. Was that her fault or their fault? She touched Mickey's arm. "How nice for you. He seems like a pleasant man, and one with his own business, too."

A silver, tinkly laugh was Mickey's response. "I suppose it was that obvious." She put her own hand through Nellie's arm and squeezed.

They walked arm in arm to the hotel. Nellie liked the feeling of having met a new friend, something she was a little short of in her Wood River valley. At the hotel, Nellie guided Mickey into the small side room where she and Sheriff Azgo had been meeting to discuss their mutual findings. The ancient cigar smell still wafted about the room like an invisible fog. They both pulled up chairs to the equally ancient parson's table.

Nell spread out the negatives and prints she had finished in the Hope Studio's darkroom. "Here is what the men looked like when they came up from below into the main hoist room." She brought out the prints. "These are prints of the ruined hoist shack on Level Thirteen." She turned to Mickey. "Have you ever been down the mine?"

"No, women aren't generally allowed. Bad luck, the men say. Plus, I can't imagine going into that deep hole in the earth. Weren't you frightened?"

Nell sat back. "Yes and no. At first, I thought I'd die of claustrophobia. It was dark and moist, and I was nervous as a cat. Then, when I began to photograph, I calmed down. That usually happens. This was much worse in some ways than the caves at Craters of the Moon."

"Craters? Where is that?"

"Our last murder investigation—"

"Murder? Is that what this is?"

Oops, thought Nellie. The sheriff would not want her to leak any secrets to anyone, let alone someone who worked at the hospital and around the injured men. "Um, no. So far, the sheriff thinks this is an accident, but the company has called in a Pinkerton detective, I think because they want to blame it on the union." She thought maybe she was digging the hole deeper.

"Craters of the Moon is a national monument in central Idaho. It is called that because it is a huge area filled with lava that spilled out of the ground over many years, and not so long ago at that. The lava left a number of caves, and I took photographs inside them." Images from that investigation still haunted Nellie.

She turned her attention to the negatives. "These must be some of the men you tend in the hospital. Do you recognize any of them?"

Mickey leaned down to study the small images of men in the mine sled. "I can't tell. Their faces are too tiny."

"You said you might have some knowledge that others don't about the explosion . . ."

"Not so much about the explosion, more about the men and what they said." Mickey touched the photograph of the twisted shack and the blackened shaft and edges on either side. The larger size print definitely was clearer than the negatives of the men. She looked up at Nell. "I'm not sure I should be repeating what I heard in the hospital and in the operating room."

Nell kept her face looking at the photographs and said nothing, waiting. She used her finger to trace the sled with the men in it, and the image of blood, broken bodies, and singed skin brought back to her the smells and horror of that day in the mine. At last, she turned her face to Mickey. "If someone did this deliberately, and I don't know that they did, we must find out who it is. If the men said anything that would be of help in the investigation, it would be important to know what it is. No one wants this to happen again. And if someone was responsible, he must pay for his crime." She watched the changing facets of Mickey's face. "You must believe that, too, don't you?"

The nurse lowered her head and, after a moment, lifted it again, determination written on her mouth and in her eyes. "Yes." She stood up, twisting her hands in anguish. "Those poor men, some of whom are so damaged they won't work again, and, of course, the ones who—" She sat down again. "Didn't survive."

Nellie desperately wanted a cup of tea, or even better, a glass of wine. Still, she didn't want to interrupt Mickey.

"They're all a little confused in my mind as we were hurrying to clean them, bandage their wounds, and so on. One man said, 'I didn't tell them. I swear to God I didn't tell them.' I don't know what he meant, and it wasn't as clear as that either. Ira said he saw someone sneaking down the drift—I guess that's a tunnel—before the explosion, and then 'all hell broke loose,' he said. His hand was burned badly and maybe a piece of something hit it, too, because it was torn up." Mickey's river of words slowed and stopped. "Accidents happen in the mine," she said, gathering speed again, "but mostly from cave-ins and timbers breaking—broken arms and legs, scrapes. There are hardly any fires down there. Why would someone do that? Even with all the explosives used in the mine, not many accidents happen with the dynamite. Sometimes, a piece of dynamite won't go off when they're blasting, and the next miner hits it with a drill, and then there's injuries. Some of the men get giant powder headaches—really bad ones from the chemicals. But having dynamite go off all on its own just doesn't happen. Or at least, it hasn't since I've been working at the hospital."

"Do you think the company would do this on purpose to get rid of the union?" Nell wanted to push that idea because Charlie had posed it.

"The company doesn't want any union members down there, and, as far as I know, there aren't. They blackball anyone with a connection to a union, even from outside like Butte, or men who lived and worked here in 1899. A few of those men are still around, although miners tend to move around a lot, going from place to place, unless they're family men." Mickey lowered her head to study the small negative of the men in the sled again.

"One man said something really strange: 'It's there, it's there. The Crystal mine.' I thought he was just out of his head. I'm not sure he said 'mine,' but I can't think what else it might have been."

"Where is the Crystal mine?" Nell hadn't heard that name, either. Many of the mines had women's names. Charlie had mentioned that some of the veins the miners followed were named after the miners themselves, or deceased miners, like the Quill vein, or names like Last Chance or Silver Dollar or Poorman. Crystal did seem odd, but, of course, that could be a woman's name.

"I have no idea," Mickey said. "I've never heard of it. There are so many claims in the area. It could be anywhere." She shook her head. "There are always rumors around town of strikes of gold or silver up in the hills. Prospectors come in and boast about rich caches and treasure hunts. Maybe there's some truth to those, but I doubt it. Even Walter gives credence to some of the rumors. I think he'd go out prospecting if he could."

"Why doesn't he?"

Mickey lifted her face to look at Nellie. "If he does, he'll find out he lost something else—me!"

Chapter Nine

"Let us take the day off in the woods," Charlie suggested at breakfast.

"All right. I could use a rest from this smelter smoke." Even as Nell answered, she coughed and then sipped her tea to soothe her throat. "How do people live here for years?"

"They get used to it. I have a possible lead to one of the stills in the woods near Burke, outside of Wallace." Charlie searched his pocket and brought out a crude drawing, like a child's version of pointed mountains, evergreen Christmas trees, and a wagon with barrels on it. "That is the real reason we are here, after all." He folded it and put it back in his pocket.

"That soda-drink store owner seemed like he would like for me to take a photo in his back room. Maybe we could stop there again?" Nellie patted Moonshine's head where he sat beside her. "Moonie could use some time outside. Can he come, too?"

Charlie scratched his ear. "We do not want to be seen entering too many illegal joints except for investigation purposes." He stood up from the table after leaving coins for the waitress. "I do not think one or two would be a problem. The main difficulty seems to be town officials who sell permits to the premises. They even have licenses of some kind on their walls. Everyone who wants liquor knows which places to frequent." He nodded toward the dog. "He will have to be on a leash." He frowned. "No, I think better not. We do not know what we will find."

Nellie sagged. Having Moonshine here in town presented problems. Maybe Rosy had wanted the company while motoring up the state. "All right. Let me take him to the Hope Studio. I think Walter will let him stay there and even take him for a walk."

The sheriff's expression was a strange one, Nellie thought. But it didn't seem fair to leave Moonie in her room while she enjoyed a picnic and being outdoors.

Once again, Charlie arranged for an automobile, and the two of them motored east to Wallace, then turned north up the river to the town of Burke. Nellie had never seen anything like it. Buildings climbed from the narrow main street up the mountainsides. In the street were a paved road and railroad tracks. She could see that if a train came through, no other vehicles or even pedestrians could be in the street, and some store awnings would have to be pulled in. At the beginning of town, the street and tracks went right through the middle of a building. "How often do trains run through here? It looks like a tight squeeze."

"It does. We are going to motor through to the other side and follow a trail from there, on foot for now." The sheriff scrunched up his shoulders as if feeling the squeeze until they reached an area where he could pull the auto off the main road. "There is an old mine up this way," he said and tapped his pocket with the amateur sketch. "Rumor is a moonshine still is hidden in it. We are going to be tourists exploring the woods for mushrooms and may stumble on it. Did you bring the basket with lunch? I will place your camera in the boot. It would look too official, I am afraid."

"Is it safe there? Losing the camera would be a complete disaster for me. Maybe I should wait here while you investigate."

"No, having you along makes it more likely we would be

taken for bumbling tourers." Charlie tucked the camera under a blanket and closed the back trunk. "I need you."

Nell rolled her eyes. "To make you look innocent?" She suppressed a smile. He would always look threatening, she surmised, although she did know he was kind and generous, but also tall and dark, and his serious face rarely softened as it had at the Basque boardinghouse in Mullan. "Smile, Sheriff. Pretend you are having a good time on an outing in the woods!"

Charlie opened his mouth and lifted the corners of his lips.

"That looks like you just ate something sour."

Then he laughed. "You see? I do need you." He slipped his arm around her waist and hugged her to him. Nellie sank into his chest, her cheek pressing against his soft flannel shirt, but he released her almost immediately.

"Here is the old road to the Constitution mine. It is too broken up to take an automobile on it, but a wagon could manage the bumps." Charlie motioned Nellie along to a road disguised as an ancient, two-rutted tracked path. It didn't look used at all, in Nellie's opinion. He pulled out the map again.

"There is also an exit from the mine that circles around to Murray. Product may go out there."

"Product meaning moonshine?"

"Yes, indeed. Remember the still at 4th of July Creek? I expect we will find something like that, maybe with just as dangerous men involved."

Patches of white clover flowers already grew where the sun shown. Its warmth was bringing out more green, and a whiff of orange wafted by. "What a heavenly aroma," Nell said, and turned around to see where it came from. Down slope from where they walked, shrubs with white blossoms crowded the open area. "Do you know what those flowers are?"

"Syringa. They grow all over Idaho. Some people call them mock orange." Even Charlie pulled in a long breath—and smiled. "Lovely, is it not?"

Nellie placed her hand through Charlie's arm and crowded close to him. "What a delicious idea to go to the woods today."

The lumpy track was harder to navigate than Nellie would have thought. Her boots helped, but she still found her ankles twisting, and she stumbled over holes and swales. Finally, she fell behind Charlie. He hiked steadily forward and seemed not to realize she wasn't with him any longer. A fallen tree resting on rocks and in front of another evergreen tree offered a place to sit, and she took it. She had been enjoying the songs of birds as she stumbled along, but, as she took the weight off her feet, she realized that the forest around them had quieted. The track curved uphill, and she could no longer see Charlie or hear him. She shivered, but not from anything cold.

Thinking she should catch up to the sheriff, Nellie sprang to her feet. At the same time, a man stepped out of the forest as silently as a ghost might. His face was obscured with a bushy beard, and a knit hat covered most of his hair. "Oh!" Nellie said. She moved one leg back and hit the log, causing her to sit again.

"Who are you, and what are you doing here?" the man growled in a back-country accent, his "you" coming out like "ya," and "here" sounding like "hyar." He took a menacing step toward her, one arm raised as if to grab her.

Nell cowered backwards. "I—we are looking for mushrooms and having a picnic." Her voice sounded squeaky to her own ears. "We thought we might find a hot springs, too."

The man stared at Nell. "Mushrooms? Ain't never heared of such a thing up here. And who is 'we'?"

"My f-friend. He's up ahead." Nellie pointed to the turn in the road. "Charlie," she called, but her voice fell flat amongst the trees.

"Ha. You look purty lonely, little gal. Mebbe I could be your friend." The man's sneer from his red mouth surrounded by hair frightened Nell even more. He lunged toward her.

"Charlie!" Nellie screamed. The man smelled of alcohol, and his breath almost scorched her skin. She scooted sideways and slapped him with her basket, a weak blow that didn't do anything but maybe spur him on. His beard scraped against her cheek.

And then a strong hand grabbed the attacker's collar and pulled him off Nellie and threw him to the ground, with no more apparent effort than a man slapping at a mosquito. "Hey! Stay away from her. What do you think you are doing?" Charlie lifted his leg to stomp on his quarry but did not. "We are out for a morning stroll. Who are you?"

The man took his time pulling himself to his feet and moved a good distance from the sheriff. "None of yer business. These woods is private property owned by the Constitution mine. You two are trespassing. Get outta here."

"There were not any signs, and I see no mine." Charlie gave an exaggerated look around and then helped Nellie to her feet, keeping an arm around her back to give her support.

"I told him we were on a picnic and looking for mushrooms or maybe a hot springs," Nell said. Her voice sounded stronger than earlier. She leaned into the sheriff's strong arm. It felt like an iron bar, and it stayed taut. He wasn't releasing his vigilance. Her fright had lifted when he pulled the man away from her. "You—you terrible man! We aren't hurting anyone or anything, just having a pleasant walk. How dare you! Wait until I tell my friends back home. They'll think this place is overrun by crazy people, like you!" She drew a kerchief from a pocket and pretended she was crying.

"Now, Cora," the sheriff said, improvising as well. "This man will not bother you anymore," he said and turned to the interloper. "Will you?" He expanded his chest, took a threatening step toward the bearded man, and raised the arm not circling Nellie.

"No. No, I'm sorry I made the little lady cry. I didn't mean to affrighten her." He turned tail and stepped back toward the forest. "I'll be agoin' now. Just stick to this track, and nobody'll bother you no more." He disappeared almost as quickly as he had appeared.

"Is he gone?" Nell whispered to Charlie.

He stepped into the woods where the man had disappeared and searched for a few moments. "Gone." He kept his voice as low as hers. "Did he hurt you?"

"No, just frightened me. He tried to attack." Or worse, she continued to herself. "Should we go back?"

"No, I caught a glimpse of some kind of workings up several bends," he said and gestured to the curve. In a louder tone, he said, "I found a pleasant meadow up ahead where we can have our picnic. I do not think we will find mushrooms today. Or hot springs?" The question was in his voice, as if to ask "whatever made you say that?"

This time, Nellie kept her hand in Charlie's arm, and he slowed to her pace. Around the corner there was indeed a pleasant small meadow where the grass was green, and a few wildflowers appeared to be nearing bloom. "Oh, this is lovely! I'm sorry I fell behind." She followed Charlie's pointed finger to catch a glimpse of the dirt tailings falling down a mountainside that were a sign of mining activity. She placed her index finger on her lips. In the quiet she heard the sound of distant men's voices and the faint *wham wham wham* of hammering or steady pounding. Again she whispered. "It does sound like some kind of work ahead."

"Stay here," Charlie ordered as he continued up the track.

"No," Nell answered. "I'm not going to be alone again." She hurried to catch up with him. He stopped, gave an exasperated sound, but began again, walking to the side of the track in the grasses. Nell followed.

Around another curve, the noises increased. The sheriff waved to Nellie to lower herself out of sight, as he took one cautious step after another to a screen of shrubs. She hastened to his side. Through the screen several men worked to disassemble what had clearly been a still and its accompanying tanks and pipes. Too bad she didn't have her camera, she thought. She could take a photograph of the evidence of moonshining. What a perfect place to make the liquor. The equipment looked as if it fit right in with a mining operation. If she hadn't known what a still looked like, she might have walked right past it. Any steam would have appeared to be coming out of the tunnel right behind it.

Charlie plucked at Nell's sleeve and motioned to go back, again leading her with quiet steps in the grass until they returned to the picnic spot. "The still will not be there much longer," he said in a quiet voice. "I am sorry we did not bring your camera, although setting it up might have been dangerous."

Nell pulled a blanket from her basket and spread it on the ground. "Let's eat. I'm hungry." She sat and pulled from the basket sandwiches purchased from the café next to the hotel, along with small glass containers and cookies wrapped in waxed paper. "We have our eye witness testimony."

The sheriff stood above her. "I think we would be wise to leave here as soon as possible. That man who attacked you warned his friends. They may come looking for us."

"Not until they have finished taking down the still. They had a ways to go. If anyone still watches us, we should act the innocents we pretend to be." She handed Charlie half a sandwich of ham and cheese. "Eat."

★ ★ ★ ★ ★

Back at the automobile, they found the doors opened and seats dislodged. Nellie gave a low scream and headed for the back end. Fortunately, Charlie had locked it. Her camera was still hidden under a blanket and appeared safe and sound. "Thank heavens!" She grabbed it up and cradled it to her chest. She turned to the sheriff. "Should we go back and try to take a photograph?"

Charlie seemed to ponder her question. He stowed the seats back in place and closed all but the front doors of the automobile. He motioned for her to get into the passenger side. When he had entered and closed the door, he said, "I think it is too dangerous, Nell. At this point, the still has probably been dismantled, and we might run into angry moonshiners." He pulled out the choke and pressed the starter button. "There will be plenty more in these woods. Next time, I will leave you at home and take either one of the revenue men or a Pinkerton, so you are not in danger."

As he turned the auto back onto the main road, Nell looked behind. Two men dashed out of the forest and ran toward them. "Hurry up! They're after us!"

Charlie peered into the side mirror and stepped on the gasoline. As one of the men tried to step on the running board, the auto jerked ahead, and he fell back, shaking his head. The other man was the bearded one who threatened Nell. When they entered town on the main road, a train appeared at the other end, headed toward them. A train's whistle blasted the air, warning them to stop or get out of the way. Charlie pulled the auto up onto the boardwalk via the ramp that led to it. Several pedestrians jumped aside, hollering at them. A storekeeper hurrying to pull an awning in, called, "You ain't safe there!"

The two men had disappeared, so Charlie jammed the auto

into reverse and tried to go back the same way he had come up. The wheels on the auto slipped off the ramp, and Nellie could feel the car tip sideways. She slid down into the foot well and grabbed the side handle. She could almost feel the train hit them and turn them into a pile of metal like the dynamited shack inside the mine. She would end up twisted like a pretzel, too. She closed her eyes and tried not to scream.

And then she heard the clank of train wheels as the engine chugged past and the rattle rattle of the cars. Charlie had managed to squeeze the auto into a space between two buildings. "You saved us," Nellie cried, as she grabbed his leg and tears sprang from her eyes. "I was sure we were dead."

Charlie heaved as well, his breath jagged. "I scraped the auto all down one side, I am afraid. I could hear the sound." He grabbed her hand and pulled her up to him. "I am so sorry, Nellie. This turned out to be a terrible day."

Nellie found herself comforting the sheriff. "It's all right. We're alive to fight another day." She smoothed his hair, hugged him around the neck. "Maybe we should get out of here." She laughed. "That reminds me, I want to go back to Mullan and Wallace and photograph the miners drinking. That would be good evidence, would it not?"

Chapter Ten

Nellie persuaded Charlie to stop at the cigar store in Mullan again. The sultry woman was not at the front counter, probably because it was still early, not even dinnertime yet. In the back room, however, there were already men with drinks. She wondered if they were not employed or had later shifts at one of the mines. The bartender was the same. He greeted Nellie with a huge grin. "I thought you forgot to come back." He looked at Charlie a little suspiciously but turned his attention back to Nell. "You can take all the pictures you want. What do you want first?"

"Thank you. What's your name?" Nellie unpacked her camera, glad it was still in one piece and not squished like a pancake. She was still a little shaky.

"Bert. Short for Albert. You know, like Prince Albert in a can. Heh heh." The man's apron might once have been white but now sported dark stains, some of which could be dried blood. His hair, a mix of gray and brown, was combed over the top of an apparently bald head from a part above his left ear. He patted the top of his head with a quick motion, maybe worried the hairs wouldn't stay in place. A gold tooth in the front of his mouth flashed as he opened and closed his jaw.

"Let me take one of you behind the bar, pouring into a glass from a bottle. Then maybe I could get a group photo of several of your customers and you, maybe toasting something." She set up her tripod and readied the camera. "It is rather dark in here.

Either everyone is going to have to be very still, or maybe we could open the curtains at the back of the room . . . ?" As she looked around, Nellie saw a paper stuck to the side of the backbar. It had the appearance of a certificate of sorts. She wanted a closer look and then was able to get one, when she moved behind the bar to adjust Bert's position. It said "City of Mullan" and more writing in small script. "Watch your bottle, not me, Bert." It was a ceramic jug, as Nell imagined a moonshine pot would appear. "A serious expression, first, then one with a smile." Bert followed Nell's instructions. She wished he had a clean apron on.

While she worked, she saw Charlie in the background, inspecting the certificate, walking to the back of the store, where he pulled shades up, wandering among mostly empty tables because their occupants had moved to the counter to watch her and Bert. After two photos of Bert, Nell asked the men to sit at the bar and hold glasses up as if they were toasting each other. She didn't know if these drinkers ever did that, but it seemed like a way to get more than one person into the photograph. She was able to include a bank of glasses and several bottles behind Bert into the photo. Without asking, she also took a photo of the back of the bar and incidentally included the certificate. The men laughed and joked among themselves. All of them were in rough clothes, and one of them wore a cap while the others were bare-headed. Mostly, they were young, unshaven, and had the look of back-country boys.

Nell took the men's names and asked where they worked or lived. All were employed at the mines near Burke—the Tiger-Poorman, the Hecla, the Hyperion. They were off shift and wanted a drink before heading to the boardinghouse "up Nine Mile," they offered.

"Do you come in every day?" Nell asked. None seemed shy about drinking, and no one mentioned the Prohibition laws, definitely not the bartender.

Nell called to Charlie to join her. She thanked the fellows, gave Bert a pat on his shoulder, and said she'd bring the photos to show when she had a chance to develop and print them up. "I'll see if I can get a Chicago newspaper to publish them. I'll do a title like 'Cigar Store in the Wild West.' Would you like that? Can I use your name, Bert?"

He blushed with all of her attention. "I guess so. Maybe only my first name, though. People back East might not reckon how we do business in the West." His laugh was slow, and he winked at her.

Outside, Charlie walked around their automobile, judging the damage from the scrape on the building in Burke. "Guess it is not as bad as I thought. Still, I may have to pay for repairs, and I am not sure the feds will reimburse me." Charlie didn't lose his glum face until they arrived in Wallace and parked along the street. The buildings erected after the big fire in 1910 were all brick and looked almost new. They reminded Nellie of the red brick buildings along model train tracks in toy stores in Chicago. It appeared Easterners did imagine how Westerners lived, maybe not the extent of the alcohol available—they would be envious—but at least what their buildings looked like: short, red, and sturdy.

A man in police-like garb watched them park their auto along the street. When Nell and Charlie climbed out, he approached Charlie. "Looks like you had an accident, mister. Are you two all right? New in town?"

Charlie appeared leery of the stranger coming up to them. "We had an accident in Burke. The train wanted the road we traveled on." He gave a short laugh.

"Do you want to report it to the local sheriff?" the man asked.

"No, I do not think so. No one was hurt. We thought we would stop in at a soft drink parlor and get a refreshment. It was a trying afternoon." Charlie held out his hand. "Thank you for your concern, though." The man ignored Charlie's offer of a shake. "Are you part of the local police? Maybe you could direct us to a place of business that welcomes women."

The man blushed. "Most women in these parts don't go in bars, er, parlors."

"Ah," Charlie said. "Maybe you could direct us to a restaurant or hotel, then, for some refreshment and perhaps a meal. We are strangers in town."

Nellie still wore her long pants from the hike in the woods. The man studied her and then blushed again. She thought he had stared too long and turned away from him. "All the women in the East wear pants now. It is the latest fashion." The man wouldn't know if she lied or not, she suspected. Anyway, her pants were much more modest than the short skirts some women wore these days. She turned back to him. "Are you the police? Or do you approach strangers in town out of curiosity?"

"Well, no. Yes. I was fired." Again, the ruddy flush moved from his neck, across his shaven cheeks, and up into his honey-colored hair. "The sheriff thought I was too strict on the soft-drink parlors and cigar stores." He removed the cap he wore, releasing a thatch of hair that needed a haircut. "They all get their licenses from the mayor's office and pay a fee. The sheriff called it a 'fine by license.' I never heard of such a thing in Washington State where I come from. Prohibition means no liquor, in my opinion."

"Does that mean you are new in town yourself?" Nellie asked. He might be a good source of information on her and Charlie's quest to get evidence for the federal marshal. "Would you like to join us?" Then she realized Charlie was shaking his head from behind the ex-policeman. She wondered why, but she had already issued the invitation. "Or perhaps you are busy?" She tried to bow out of her invite.

"There's a good eating place in the Wallace Hotel, right around the corner. I could sit with you a spell. Are you from Washington, too?"

Charlie stepped in. "No, we are from south Idaho. I am a sheriff from Blaine County." He pulled out his badge. "I do not want you to think I am hiding my identity. I am here investigating the situation with bootleggers at the request of the federal marshal."

Nellie rolled her eyes. Now what kind of information would they get? She walked between the two men to the restaurant. Both were tall. Both had to shorten their steps to let her keep up. She wondered if all lawmen were tall in the West. The sheriff opened the door, and Nellie and their new acquaintance stepped through.

"My name is Matt Wooden," said the fired policeman. "What are yours?"

The sheriff used his full name, and Wooden goggled. He didn't try to repeat it.

"I'm C. N. Burns," said Nellie. "I'm a photographer. I work for the sheriff here."

Once seated, Nellie decided to keep the conversation going. "What did you do that got you, uh, fired?" Maybe she was too blunt, she thought. She could feel Charlie squirm beside her.

"I arrested a bartender for serving liquor." He paused. "And three men for buying liquor and a woman for selling herself." He directed all of this to Charlie, not Nellie. "Apparently, it's all right to drink liquor, buy liquor, and who—er, sell—er, prostitute oneself in this town." His blush seemed a permanent fixture on his face.

"It is a mining town, you know," Nellie said. "You must be from a city in Washington."

"Seattle." The man sat quiet for a minute. "I was let go there, too. I arrested some Chinamen for gambling. Hard to know all the local rules, I guess. My police academy instructors would be appalled at what goes on here in the northwest."

Charlie had been nodding his head, as if in agreement. "You went to an academy in the East? Surely, there are speakeasies and brothels there."

"I grew up in California and went to school there. Wish I'd stayed. Guess I'll go back." He drummed his fingers on the table. "What would you do?"

"I would go back to the police chief and ask for his advice." Charlie's mouth twitched. "I suspect you might have argued with him. Probably not a politic thing to do in a town like this."

Nellie decided not to say anything. Maybe Charlie was correct, although she knew she would have argued herself and probably been fired, too. All this law breaking would have been a lot to bear to a graduate of a police academy bent on enforcing the law. It was sometimes hard for her, too, even though she hadn't gone anywhere to learn about the law. She was learning from Charlie, though, and realized what was "right," wasn't always the best thing to do.

"All these bars—er, parlors, or whatever they are—they buy a license to serve liquor. How can you do that in Prohibition? Paying fines in advance? Sounds like corruption to me." Matt Wooden sat straighter in his chair. "Or bribes." Drum, drum, drum with his fingers. "Isn't it? Can you arrest anyone—maybe the mayor?" His voice grew louder as he talked. People at other tables glanced their way.

"Calm down, Matt," Charlie said. "I am investigating, not making arrests. Where does the money go, do you know?" He kept his voice low and level.

Food and soft drinks, tea for Nellie, arrived. No one spoke until the waitress left the table.

"Who knows? No one here lives a high life, including the mayor or any of the police. If they're getting extra money, they don't show it. Not that I can see. Maybe they're squirreling it away to have a high old time someplace else." His voice lowered to a whisper. "The chief said the licenses paid for extra duty police in case of trouble. Seeing as how half those miners are dead drunk by closing time, and we—I mean they—have to visit the houses once or twice a night to calm things down, that may be true. Still don't make it right."

The sheriff nodded his head again. "How about other crimes? Are they being ignored?"

Matt tilted his head one way and then another. "Well, no. We—they don't have that many crimes. It's a small town. One murder of a moonshiner we been working on, but no one seemed upset about it. Little wonder. His moonshine probably killed a couple miners. Pure poison." He slurped on the stew he had ordered and stopped talking.

"That wasn't right, either, was it?" Nell said. "Who extracted the revenge?"

"We—they think it was the brother of one of the miners. They don't know yet." He put his fork and spoon down—a two-fisted eater. "I don't think it was the brother. I think it was another bootlegger." He stared at Charlie. "I could work on that crime, couldn't I?" He pulled the napkin from his neck. "Would you come with me to the station and talk to the chief? Maybe he would assign me to help you." He stood up. "That is, if you'd need some help."

Nellie was fairly certain Charlie did not want to be identified to the local police, as they might be involved in corruption. That was one of the things he was investigating, even if he said he was not. She was surprised when he stood up to accompany Matt Wooden.

"You wait here, Miss Burns. I will return after I talk some more with Mr. Wooden." Charlie placed his napkin next to a near-empty plate of steak and eggs. "I will not be long."

Nellie pondered the fine by license system that seemed to prevail in the two towns they were supposed to investigate. If nobody was profiting from the scheme, maybe it didn't really matter. Except it was still a violation of Prohibition. If someone were caught distilling liquor, moonshining, and hadn't paid the license, he would probably be arrested, convicted, and spend time in jail. It sounded, though, as if the soft-drink dealers were the ones who paid their fines in advance. She wondered if Charlie would ask about the moonshiners. Did they get the opportunity to pay fines in advance?

The sheriff returned and sat down next to Nellie. "Our former policeman was a fount of knowledge," he said. "I hope he gets his job back." He ordered another cup of coffee. "The dead bootlegger drowned, he said. The man who found him pulled him out of the river. There was a question about the good Samaritan's name: John Smith. Matt Wooden said he has disappeared, or, at least, no one in town has found him—nor have the police in Mullan or Bitterroot. Wooden doubts the name is real, and he wonders if 'John Smith' actually did murder the bootlegger."

"Where was the body found?" Nell surprised herself at being so matter of fact about a potential murder. Perhaps because the men who died or were hurt in the mine were so much worse off, and this one seemed like a newspaper article—cold and old news.

"That is what Matt found strange. John Smith said the man drowned in one of the streams up above Burke. Mostly, they are fairly small—hard to drown in. Still, it is spring, and snow melt can turn some of them into minor floods on the way down the mountains." He sipped his coffee and held his cup with both hands. "Maybe this is why the police in the valley do not seem energized to find a potential killer. It was a bootlegger, apparently from one of the other closed mine operations, the Success," he said and gave a wry smile. "So much for Success."

Nellie sighed. "Let's go back to Bitterroot. I want to visit one of the brothels, see what I can learn there about the mine explosion." She never, ever thought she would say she wanted to visit a house of prostitution.

Chapter Eleven

Of course Nell knew about brothels. Even, and maybe especially, Chicago had them. So did Hailey, Idaho, but nothing like this one. Here she was in this rugged mining town standing in front of a house of prostitution. The tragedy in the mine had reminded her of the bloody scenes in meat-packing plants. Only here, they were men, not destined to be eaten. Still, the maw of the mine adit could be thought of that way, especially by wives and mothers. Again, she had left Moonie behind, this time asleep in her room. They had taken a long morning walk.

With visions of white slavery in her head, Nellie knocked on the door of what looked like a once elegant hotel. Nothing. She knocked again. Maybe one simply walked in. She took a deep breath, tried to stand three inches taller than she really was, wrapped her scarf tighter around her neck, and opened the door.

Inside, there was no one in the entry area. What did she expect? It was ten in the morning. A large painting of Leda and the Swan covered one wall. Across from the painting, a standing desk barred the way to a double doorway, its paneled doors closed.

Nell crept toward the doors and put her ear against a panel. At first, she heard nothing, then high heels striding toward her. She jumped back, but not quite fast enough to look innocent of eavesdropping, as one of the doors opened.

Gray eyes on a woman about her size, maybe an inch smaller,

stared at Nell. She shivered. Those eyes were cold as the spring rain outside.

"May I help you?" Her voice matched her eyes.

"Yes," Nell said, "I mean, that is, if you are . . ." She couldn't remember the woman's name for a half second. The stories about her floated with Nell's memory. "Yes, if you are Mimi McConnell. I am looking for information about Izzie Savich."

"He's upstairs, either passed out cold, or dead."

As shocked as Nellie was at that news, she did remember there was something she was taught growing up in Chicago. When someone appears to have died, check for a pulse or a breath with a mirror. Her mother taught her that. It came in useful when Nell photographed dead people.

"I can have someone roust him out. What do you want with him?" Mimi, as Nell thought of her, stood behind the podium-like desk.

"He gave us information about the mine explosion last week. I wanted to check it out with him again. He said he wasn't working that day, but he seemed to be familiar with what happened." Nellie felt as if she were floundering, not really getting to the point of her search for the man. The sheriff hadn't been much more specific, either. He was the one who talked with Izzie in the café near the hotel, and then again later, seeking information about being in the mine itself, before Charlie went down as a prospective mucker. This day, he was out searching the hills farther east, looking for stills again after their somewhat aborted adventure near Burke. She hoped the Pinkerton detective accompanied him. He knew better than to go it alone. Nellie turned her attention back to Mimi, who still waited for Nellie to say more.

When she didn't, Mimi asked, "And who are you?" There was nothing in her appearance to suggest she was the madam of this house. Her hair was dark, much like Nell's, but much longer and wrapped to look shorter. Her dress, a deep navy blue, fit her well and had the look of a business outfit with its neat white dickey and white cuffs. Nell almost felt untidy next to her with her own everyday dress and wind-blown hair.

Nell could be friends with this woman, she thought, although Mimi was quite a bit older, maybe over forty. She didn't look it, except for the few gray strands in her hair and telltale wrinkles around her mouth. She didn't appear to smile much.

"I am accompanying Sheriff Asteguigoiri from Blaine County, Idaho. We have been asked by the mining company to look into the explosion and see if we can find whether someone purposely caused it, or if it was an accident." Nellie decided not to mention the investigation into the Prohibition problem. Presumably, a brothel would be serving liquor to its customers, at least that was apparently what occurred in the other towns in the valley. "I am a photographer from the same area." She couldn't decide whether to disclose that she worked for the sheriff. It would seem odd that they were in Bitterroot at the same time, unless they were investigating another crime. "My name is Nellie Burns." Already, she might have said too much about Izzie. She would wait and see to disclose anything else.

A flicker of a smile ghosted around Mimi's lips. "Ah. I have heard of both of you." She lowered her head for a moment, possibly studying the large ledger book that lay open on the tall desk. When she again faced Nellie, her face had relaxed. "Come with me," she said and turned back to the double doors, opening one of them.

When Nellie entered the main part of the house, she saw a large saloon area, an upright piano, and what appeared to be a dance floor to the left. In the wall to her right, a door stood open, and she peered into a room like a men's club: large, comfortable chairs with ottomans, a pool table, a discreet bar at the opposite side of the room. The lingering aroma of pipes or cigars wafted toward her, for once a pleasant smell. She could see herself settling into one of the chairs with her feet on an ottoman and a nap coming on. The colors were cocoa brown, beige, and amber, soothing in their depth, a brown study in fact. She wondered how many liaisons or business deals had been clinched here. More likely, deals of a more erotic sort.

Mimi ushered Nell into the club room. "Wait here, and I will see what I can find out about Izzie. If he woke up, he may have left already. Would you like tea?"

"Oh yes, very much," Nell answered. She wanted to ask Mimi a dozen questions about the house, about her role, and about her history. The madam breathed history, Nell thought, and mystery. She glanced around, and a game table, maybe a gambling table, filled one corner. Nell decided to sit in one of the upright chairs close to it. A club chair seduced her, but she would have none of it. This was a business visit and not a leisurely sop to her curiosity.

The house was deadly quiet. No sounds penetrated from outside, although a busy street ran alongside. Gradually, Nell heard muffled voices, women's voices, that seemed to pass through several doors from the inner portion of the structure, maybe from a kitchen, she decided. Occasionally, she heard a step or two upstairs, but nothing loud, more like slippers whispering across a bare floor. She decided to investigate, not snoop, she told herself, the room and beyond. The bar itself was empty of whiskey, beer bottles, even wine bottles. If anything forbidden was served there, it was not in sight at the moment. Glasses of various kinds reflected by a back mirror shone in the room's light coming from a chandelier composed of crystal drops and round light bulbs. Wall sconces held candles for a more romantic scene, probably used at night. There was a farther room, but Nellie didn't have a chance to explore before a woman arrived with a tray, teacups, and teapot, as well as slices of pound cake and small biscuits.

"Miss Burns? I'm Victoria. Mimi asked me to bring refreshments to you." She placed the tray on the gambling table. "Shall I pour?" She almost curtsied, an odd effect in a house with its reputation.

"Thank you, Victoria. I'm Nell. How kind of her. Is she returning?" She re-sat herself at the table. "Yes, please. It is so chilly outside, although this room is certainly warm and cozy."

"Yes, it is a room for special guests." Victoria, much taller than Mimi and rounder and softer looking, lifted her lips in a sly smile. "They don't often drink tea, though." She poured the tea, then covered her lips with fingers tipped in bright-red nail polish. "Of course, I shouldn't say that," she whispered. "You might be a revenuer."

Nell could feel herself blush. Victoria didn't know how close she was to the truth. Nell wanted to say, *your secret is safe with me,* but did not dare do so. Victoria left, and Nell sipped her tea. After a short wait, Mimi appeared again. She, too, sat at the gaming table, poured herself some tea, and studied Nell.

"Tell me about your photography. Do you work alone?"

"Yes, except for the crime photography I am doing for the sheriff from Blaine County. Otherwise, I am trying to work up my own portfolio of photographs, primarily landscapes, but also people. I've discovered the people photographs can be more interesting than anything else. Would your employees like to be photographed?"

Mimi seemed to almost lose her sip of tea. She held a napkin over her mouth, but it appeared to Nellie that she might be smiling behind the cloth. Brief laugh wrinkles showed around her eyes and then disappeared.

"What do you do with the photographs?"

Nellie sighed. "I have submitted several to a gallery in San Francisco, which accepted two of them for showing. One was of miners in the Triumph Mine, and the second was of a woman preparing a pie. Otherwise . . ." She shrugged her shoulders. "I would like to get several published in Chicago newspapers, where I used to live. Women journalists aren't exactly welcome anywhere." Mimi might be familiar with that attitude herself on different counts. Women who took care of themselves, in one form or another, were hardly accepted anywhere. "I did do a series for the railroad in my area to be used on tourism brochures. They showed the majestic Sawtooth Mountains and captured the sheepherding aspects in central Idaho—the sheep camps, the sheepherders, the sheep, a cowboy, and a saloon girl. I did get paid for those. Otherwise, I have a studio in Hailey and perform portrait photography for clients."

Mimi nodded her head. "Men's work and women's work. Your photographs." She moved her intense gaze away from Nellie's face. "I'll ask the girls. Women's work, too," she added. She stood up and wandered near the window. "I came from the East as well, even farther east than you did. Here we are, two eastern women, in small towns in Idaho. I sell women's bodies, and apparently you sell men's and women's faces. Not so different." She turned back to Nellie. "And maybe we both deal with corruption, one way or another." She sat in her chair again. After a moment of quiet, she said, "Nell Burns, I have some advice for you. Take it or leave it. The officials in the towns here in this silver valley are heavily involved in the sale of liquor in violation of the Prohibition laws. Be careful. Do not believe what the police tell you. They already know you are here to investigate the moonshiners and therefore understand you will suspect them, as you should. If your sheriff is also investigating the mine explosion, he must be careful. Mine accidents happen all the time, and, mostly, they are just accidents. But not always. Especially with the ongoing war between the Gem Company and the union."

Nellie was not certain how to respond. She appreciated the warning. "Why are you telling me this?" She gestured toward the bar. "It is clear that you, too, are violating the Prohibition laws and could wind up being part of our investigation."

"True," Mimi said. "But I only serve real liquor from Canada and homemade beer and wine from local producers. No jail could hold everyone who drinks liquor in this area. You must find the moonshiners and the officials who take their bribes. I definitely pay bribes to the local police, but not for liquor." For the first time, she flashed a genuine smile. "To keep my girls out of jail. We have a cozy arrangement that suits everyone."

Victoria came to the door again. "Izzie left. He didn't want to speak to anyone."

Looking from Victoria to Mimi and back, Nellie asked, "Was he here the early morning of the explosion? That would have been last . . . Friday morning, I believe. We went into the mine as the injured men were being brought to the main tunnel."

"Vickie, check the ledger, would you?" The two women in the club room waited in silence.

Victoria came back to the door and shook her head. "He came in early in the evening and then left again. I remember. He drank in the saloon, had an argument with one of the other men—a union man, I believe—created a stir, and then left, probably around the time the swing shift ended, because I heard the shift change whistle blowing." She stepped into the room, her dress a simple shift. Nothing about her advertised her profession. Maybe she wasn't a prostitute, Nellie thought. Maybe she was a secretary or housekeeper or cook, although she didn't look like any one of those kinds of worker. "Is there anything else I can get the two of you?"

When Mimi shook her head, Victoria left the room with a backward glance at Mimi. Some silent communication seemed to pass between them. "Your tea will be cold. Perhaps you would like to come another time with your camera, maybe your dog, and the sheriff. He would be quite welcome here in the club room. Victoria is the hostess here."

Nellie would have given anything to will away the hot blush she felt in her face at Mimi's words. "If your girls will let me take their photographs, I certainly will come with my camera," she said, trying to sound like a professional photographer. "I am at the Callahan Hotel. Could you leave word there for me? I think the sheriff and I will be making some forays into the areas around Wallace and Mullan. The old mines seem to be a hotbed of stills." She could bite her tongue for being so talkative, trying to cover her embarrassment at the blush. "Thank you for your advice, Mimi. I will pass it along to Char—Sheriff Azgo."

Once again, Mimi flashed the smile that appeared so rarely. "I rarely have another woman I can talk with, woman to woman. Come again any morning. Monday morning works best for my girls, if they do indeed want photographs taken. I suspect they will. Even I might succumb. Aren't we all a little vain?" She gestured toward the door and walked Nellie to the front door. She laid her hand on Nellie's arm. "I wish you well, in all your endeavors."

"And you, Mimi." Nellie bowed her head to the madam of the house, opened the front door, glanced again at Leda and the Swan. She turned back to Mimi. "One more question, please. Do the managers or supervisors come to . . ." she said and gestured to the double doors.

"Yes. There are fewer of them, and many have families. But some are single and others are . . ." Mimi raised her eyebrows and let that sentence drift off.

Nellie nodded and left. She would return if she could, maybe try to get names. But she had no intention of telling Charlie that he would be welcome, too.

Chapter Twelve

Charlie, Nell, and Rosy had decided on a method to relay messages. If Rosy wanted to talk to Nell or Charlie, he would leave a note for Nell at the front desk. If Nell or Charlie wanted to contact Rosy, Nell would leave a note for Rosy at the Café and Inn, until he moved to a boardinghouse. As he didn't want to stay in Bitterroot for more than a week, he probably would not make that move, but it was still a possibility. There was a local public telephone exchange where Rosy could telephone his boys in Hailey. Charlie said the federal marshal's office would reimburse him for the charges for his stay in town.

Charlie backed off on taking a job as a mucker now that Rosy had arrived. Instead, he spent more of his time working on the moonshine operation in Shoshone County, visiting more soft drink parlors in Mullan, Wallace, and Bitterroot. He was not the only person investigating the liquor trade, he found. A revenuer from a federal office in Seattle made himself known to Charlie by following him clumsily as Charlie poked around the back country roads. At one point, Charlie had hidden himself in an abandoned shack and waited for the man. When the man passed by, Charlie stepped out, his revolver in his hand.

"Who are you and why are you following me?" The sheriff didn't actually point his weapon at the man, who was almost as tall as Charlie, clean shaven, and wore cowboy boots, an anomaly in this mining area. Nevertheless, the man eyed the gun and raised his hands.

"Whoa. I'm no threat to you, Sheriff. We're in the same business." The man's hands were clean and clear of calluses and bruises, and in combination with the cowboy boots told Charlie he was no miner. "I don't have a weapon. Can I lower my hands?"

Charlie nodded. Unlike most of the people in the area, this man had no touch of an accent from a foreign land. The sheriff still held his weapon and waited.

"I'm Julius Weber. I work for the federal government, a revenuer, in the common parlance. I understand you are, too. I wanted to be sure you were on the up and up, so I've been watching you and your photographer friend. She's a sweet little package."

Charlie felt an instant rage at the insult to Nell. He hoped he didn't show his reaction. "Cora Nell Burns is my employee, not a 'package.' " He kept himself from pointing his revolver directly at the man opposite him. "Where's your badge?"

Weber eased one of his hands into the jacket he wore and brought out a federal agent identification card. He held it out for inspection. Charlie took it and studied it closely. He was not familiar with all the federal agencies that might be involved in a Prohibition violation, but the card appeared to be legitimate. He allowed himself to relax and stuck his revolver into the back of his waistband under his own jacket.

"Can I see yours?" Weber asked.

"No, I do not have one. I am not an official federal agent. I am Sheriff Azgo, a county sheriff, brought in by the federal marshal in Idaho to investigate. The marshal does not trust local law enforcement and, for all I know, does not trust any other agents, either. I am on my way to seek out another still, based on a tip from an informer. These 'tips' have not often been reliable. I have run into difficulties more than once."

"Are you wanting to arrest the moonshiners? That's my job,

you know." The agent took his identification back and stuffed it in his pocket. "That and arresting the buyers, meaning the 'soft-drink' parlor owners. We intend to put a stop to these scofflaws."

Charlie wished he had known about this revenuer. He wondered how many more were involved in the area. "I am trying to find the source of the scofflaws, as you call them. The bootleggers are successful because none of the powers-that-be care anything about enforcing the laws, hence all the parlors and the brothels who serve liquor. I want to know who is behind all the operations, including whether the local police, the town officials, or others are in on the deals. I don't want any raids until I find out."

"And let those drunks continue to flail outside the parlors and brothels? Sorry, no can do. We can aim most of our efforts at the bootleggers. Why don't you concentrate on the 'city fathers'?" Weber quit standing and sat on a stump, one still covered with the remains of the huge 1910 burn.

"Is that why you are up here, too? Are you looking for stills, or are you just following me?" Charlie didn't warn the agent about the black soot on the stump. That was the agent's lookout. He did admire the cowboy boots, though. They were tooled with a design of a horse's head and colored in with red and blue. They did make Weber look like a city dandy posing as a horseman.

"Wanted to see what you were doing. I figured you were after a still when you took off into this backcountry, and maybe you managed to squirrel some information from someone in town. Did you?" Weber finally noticed his pants were getting covered with charcoal black. He stood and swiped his hand across his butt, trying to clean himself off.

"Why don't we move forward together. Better to have two of us if we do find something." The sheriff tried not to grin at the agent's attempt to sweep off ashes. "If you are intent on a raid, then I can keep watch while you go back to get your fellow conspira—revenuers to knock over the moonshine operation and arrest the scofflaws." He headed on up the trail and left the agent to decide for himself. After a few minutes, he heard the man scrabbling behind him to catch up.

The two men followed an abandoned road that reflected use, but not much. Charlie noticed a white animal skeleton, head and ribs, off to one side, apparently abandoned by a hunter in the past. The cowboy boot heels didn't support the man well, because he slid and stumbled, creating more noise than any animal would. The sheriff stopped, shaking his head. "You make too much noise. Wait here, while I scout ahead. If there is anything around the next bend, I will come back and alert you. Otherwise, no bootlegger is going to hang around while we scare off birds, animals, and what-all with all your scraping and tumbling." He continued on, and Weber did not join him.

Glad to be alone again, Charlie appreciated the faint rustle of aspen leaves and the chuckling creek nearby. This country contained so much more water than the high desert he was used to. He paused several times but heard no mechanical sounds at all. The abandoned Success Mine he was seeking had failed several years ago, according to Matt Wooden, the ex-policeman. Charlie had asked Mikel about it, but he said he knew of no moonshining business in the surrounding countryside; all he knew about were abandoned mines and one or two logging camps. Charlie had taken the information, knowing those sites would all provide excellent places for clandestine operations. He side-stepped into the forest along the track, making as little sound as he could. Amber evergreen needles cushioned the ground, helping his stealthy search. He sniffed the air, hoping to smell the fruits of a distillery. Evergreen trees, white bark of aspens, mottled cottonwood trunks, and ripening salmon berries were all he identified.

A few more steps, he thought, and then he would give it up. And then he heard the jangling of an animal's bridle. He stepped deeper into the forest, hiding himself behind one of the larger evergreens, waiting to see if an animal appeared on the track. With cautious movements, he advanced parallel to the track until he spotted what had once been a mining operation. Two mules, the source of the jangles, grazed a distance from him. Steam arose from a mine adit, not necessarily a sign of mining. He waited and watched. Soon, a man appeared in the entrance and loaded up short wood pieces and re-entered the dark hole in the mountain. Charlie moved closer, continuing to use shrubs to shield himself. A wagon to one side of the mine adit contained a load of ceramic containers—jugs. Clearly, this was a moonshine operation. Judging by the number of jugs in the wagon, it was also a successful operation. Now, what he needed to do was to follow the wagon and mules to their destination and tie this operation to specific locations back in the valley. It was not an easy task on foot, not even in his auto. Once he knew the direction of the wagon, he could conjecture the location of the exit from the mountains. He decided to enlist the revenuer to assist him in this end of the investigation, even though he was still uncertain that he could trust Julius Weber, if that was truly his name.

With as much speed as he could manage and still move without disturbing either the shrubbery or the ground beneath him, Charlie stepped away from his viewpoint. Once the mine was no longer visible, he hurried without so much caution. Around two bends, he found Weber, lounging against a tree, smoking a cigarette.

"I found the still at the Success Mine," Charlie said. "I want to try and follow the transfer of moonshine to its ultimate buyer. I need you to keep an eye on what goes on here, after I figure out in what direction the transport will go." He gestured with his head back toward the mine. "Come with me. You can serve a purpose, and, once the product is gone, you can alert your agents and raid the place for all I care."

Weber ground out his cigarette, at least taking care it was completely out in bare ground, to Charlie's relief. A fire would be a disaster in these woods, still recovering from the big burn fifteen years ago that destroyed millions of acres in no more than a few days. Wood structures abounded in all the small mining towns around, including the concentrators and other mine buildings stair-stepping up the hills. The agent sighed. "All right. Show me the way."

"And take care with where you step. The tree needles cushion the ground for the most part." Charlie led Weber through the forest to the watching spot. At last, the revenuer showed some enthusiasm for the project, keeping behind the veil of greenery and making himself comfortable. He still fell from time to time and once muttered an expletive.

Both men waited until two men carried out jug after jug and loaded them into the wagon. They hitched the mules, and one of the men climbed up to sit on the wagon. Charlie motioned to Weber that he was going to follow the wagon down the road and then return to his automobile. It was no easy task, he found. The rutted road the moonshine transport followed wound up and down in the hilly track and eventually entered an area where there were few trees or shrubs to shield him. At that point, he angled back toward where his automobile waited and left the man, mules, and wagon to wend their way down to customers.

Charlie guessed where they might reappear and tried to find a road in the same general direction where he could follow in his automobile. Eventually, he hit the end of the road and had to turn around. Once again, he wished he had Nell's expertise to photograph the location and the product so he could identify the illicit liquor in its jugs in a parlor in one of the towns. He rested his head on his hands on the steering wheel. One dead end after another. He realized he did not care deeply about catching moonshiners or liquor sellers or buyers. They could all go to hell their own way. He was far more concerned about who exploded the dynamite in the mine and killed and injured a half-dozen men. Contrary to his earlier thinking, he welcomed the revenuer and any other agents he brought with him. With numbers, it would be simpler to find the "scofflaws" as Weber called them. Charlie could turn his and Nell's efforts back to the mine investigation. Preventing further death and injury from sabotage presented a much clearer path to law enforcement than did liquor laws.

Chapter Thirteen

Nell took Moonshine in a different direction in her morning walk. She did not want to run into the same man who accosted her earlier. She also wanted to learn more about the town's layout and people. This time, she exited the side door but walked around to the main street, a long one that angled up and toward what she thought were more mining operations, maybe an abandoned one since the main tunnel was to the west. She didn't want to go there, either.

The rain from previous days had blown away, and the dawn promised a nice morning. Puddles still marked the street and sidewalk, a bumpy affair where she had to watch her step. Moonshine sniffed his way along beside her. She wanted to find a grassy field of some sort, not wanting him to leave a mess where people would walk, so she headed down a side street leading to a few more places of business and the post office, but also houses. Nearly all the houses sported vestibules in front, probably cold entrances for winter days. Some had porches extending along their fronts facing the streets, but those were few. One large house resembled what Nell thought of as European style with stucco surface and a pale color with a tile roof, maybe Mediterranean. Another resembled a country English home. They must belong to owners who had more money than most of the people in the town. Mine owners or managers, she imagined. She wished she had her camera, but she had grown tired of always humping it along on her back. A vacant field with greening grass beginning to grow tall gave Moonshine a chance to sniff his way around to relieve himself. Side streets gave away to dusty gravel in many cases, so Nell and Moonshine found their way back to Main Street.

One storefront revealed a library, just opening. A woman with white hair wound around her head, ending in a lovely pile on top of her head, smiled at the two. "Would you like to come in? Is your dog behaved? If so, he is welcome, too."

Nellie had not planned to stop anywhere, but she decided to look around at the books. Two walls were filled, and four or five shorter shelves marched up the middle of the space. She tied Moonshine to one of the chairs at a table near the front window and wandered back and forth. She had not read a book in a while and missed doing so. Her mother and she had shared loaned books in their apartment in Chicago. Her mother was a librarian herself and would be disappointed that Nellie had failed to keep up her reading habits. Borrowing a book in Bitterroot didn't seem the right thing to do, as Nellie had work to do with photography, and she didn't know how long she would be in town.

"Are you a reader?" asked the woman who had opened the door. "I am Mrs. Green, the librarian."

"I'm Nell Burns. My mother is a librarian in Chicago. I used to read quite a lot, but now I spend more time photographing."

"How nice. Do you know Mr. Barnard in Wallace? He is quite the photographer, too."

"I have heard his name. Perhaps I should visit him. I have visited the photography studio here in town—the Hope Studio. Mr. Hope was very helpful to me."

"Oh yes. I heard we had a young man here. Mr. Barnard is quite famous, with all his experience. I think he is looking for assistance from a new photographer. Maybe you would like to work for him."

"I don't think so. I don't live here. I am from central Idaho—Hailey and Ketchum. Have you heard of them?"

"Oh yes, sheep towns aren't they? I think their mining disappeared. Not like here." A somewhat self-satisfied smile lurked around Mrs. Green's lips. "We are definitely an up and coming town. The richest silver mine in the country is just down the road. And the Gem Mining Company is forward looking, what with its smelter and new zinc plant. I think we are one of the most advanced mining areas in the country." She carried several books in her arms and slipped them into the shelves.

"Sheep are a major industry in Ketchum and the mountains around the town," Nell said, wanting to defend her choice of residence. "Do you know anything about the mine accident the other day in the Gem?" She did not want to get into a "my town is better" discussion. Ketchum was so denuded of business, there was little to brag about but sheep.

The librarian finished shelving the books and faced Nellie. "Terrible, wasn't it? I heard it wasn't an accident, that a union man set it up to make Gem look bad and stop production. Gem doesn't like the union, you know. The company thinks all union members are Bolsheviks, connected to the Western Miners, the Wobblies. They're a terrible group. They go on strike and try to shut down all the mining operations."

"Then where would the men work if all the mines shut down? That doesn't make any sense. Maybe they want to be paid a fair wage instead." Nellie had lived long enough in Chicago to know all the stories about unions, including that the Wobblies were the International Workers of the World not the Western Miners Federation, and how they were out to ruin the economy. Eugene Debs, a famous union organizer there in years past, was even thrown in jail. "Or perhaps want safer working conditions. I would think they definitely want their jobs. They have families to support." Nell thought the librarian had the union groups mixed up. She supposed they were equally anathema to the mining companies.

"Most of the men are just tramp miners. They go from place to place, stirring up trouble. They work for a few days, then drink their wages and move on." The librarian straightened her shoulders and turned back to her desk, as if dismissing Nellie, perhaps regretting asking her into the library.

"I was at the hospital a few days ago. All I saw were families with children, waiting to be taken care of. I also saw some of the injured miners. I doubt they wanted the explosion," Nellie said. But maybe one of them did and had not intended getting hurt with all the others. "Do you know any of the injured miners?"

"I doubt it. I don't think any of them read."

Nellie sighed. What sort of a librarian was so prejudiced? "Thank you for inviting me into your library. And Moonshine, too. I think we'll be going now."

"Moonshine? You named him after liquor? Oh my!"

"No, I named him after how the moon shines on snow at night and creates dark shadows. I don't suppose you would understand that." Now, who was being prejudiced, Nellie thought. She opened the door and left the library. What a combination of people she had met so far in Bitterroot. So far, she liked the local madam the best, and Mickey, and Ira.

Nell decided a walk along the river might be pleasant, even if the water was gray and turbid. She headed downhill from Main Street and traveled along a path that led east, toward Wallace, away from the local Gem mine. The way was overgrown and ambled up and down along a large pipe running from east to west, held up by wood supports. She wondered if it held water. It seemed too large for anything else.

Moonie rambled along, smelling at grass and shrubs, a few

pieces of trash—bottles and cans and newspapers. Nell had released the leash but decided to hook it back up. When she stood up again, she saw two men scurrying along a path on the other side of the river. They were carrying a large box between them and looked out of place. Their clothes were dirty, and both wore what Nellie was identifying as mining caps, not tin hats, but knitted hats pulled down fairly low above their eyes. They wore the jackets Nellie thought of as "diggers." One sported a brown beard, unkempt. The other walked with a sort of hitch, although their trail must have been uneven. Nor were they enjoying the morning as she was. They kept looking behind themselves, as near as she could tell, but not across the river at her or anything on her side. Farther along on their side loomed a pile of tailings, a sure sign of mining activity. The area around Hailey contained many such telltale signs of an abandoned mining claim.

These tailings began about one-quarter up the steep side hill and extended almost down to the river. They looked like fresh, dark soil, but the rains could have caused the deep coloring. At the top of the tailings, she thought she could see the outlines of a cave. The men's actions were so suspicious looking, she decided to back up and cross the bridge to see if she could see what they were doing. It was a bit of a hike, but she didn't have any place else to go until later. She hoped to visit Mimi's place of business to take photographs there, if she could. Her appointment at the Hope Studio was not until early afternoon. She planned on printing the negatives of the injured miners on the sleds in the mine and developing the photographs of the bartender and miners in Wallace. She had left her camera pack behind this morning, wanting to enjoy the walk with Moonshine and not think about photography, especially crime photography.

The bridge itself trembled in the gush of water below it. The wood structured siding belied any strength, but automobiles, bicycles, and people traveled across seemingly without worrying about its stability. Nellie decided she would hurry to the other side and not worry either, too much. At the bridge end, she turned toward where she had seen the men, past a few yet unopened businesses and dark houses, and found an old two-track similar to others she and Charlie had explored—once a road perhaps but abandoned on account of a newer road closer to the river. If the water flooded, the new road would probably fall in, she guessed, glad to be higher on the hillside. Heavy rains the past day and night coursed like small rivers down the steep hillside, and rocks tumbled along with the flow. The slurry mess stayed mostly in ditches beside her track, but mud built up on her boot bottoms, making walking strenuous and unstable. Moonshine frolicked beside her, apparently happy not to be riding in an automobile for hours on end or sleeping in the hotel room. The glow of the sun rising turned mud puddles into brief gleaming copper coins before they returned to the reality of sludge.

This is probably a mistake, Nell thought. She saw no other people along the track, but she could hear morning sounds behind her of auto horns, truck rumbles, and the bump of both crossing the bridge. Shrub leaves glistened like prisms. She stopped to hear any signs of the men ahead, but only bird song filtered through the air. Other than the mud caking on her boots, it was a pleasant walk, so she decided to continue on to the end of a ridge sloping down to the water and then turn around. She released Moonshine's leash so he could wander as he wanted.

At the bend of the ridge, she slowed and again searched along the path ahead. The mine tailings dropped to an enclosure of a patch of small trees and shrubs. And there was a cave, a dark, yawning hole at the top. She saw motion in the thick bushes clinging to the hillside. By now, she, as well as the men ahead of her, if they lingered, were hidden from the view of the lower roadway by rocks and greenery. She glanced down to the river. She had been steadily climbing so that now the spring runoff raged yards below her. Her perch no longer felt stable. She grabbed at a syringa's branches to steady herself, at the same time breathing in the lush aroma of orange.

Moonshine barked and then growled. He leaped ahead toward the motion in the shrubs.

"What is it, Moonie? Is there an animal over there?" She scraped each of her boots on a rock, released her bush, and made her way after him. All she had ever seen in this area were deer and a few elk, so she didn't worry about a possible conflict between Moonshine and something bigger—a bear or mountain lion. They wouldn't approach so close to town, she thought. Her dog dashed into the shield of shrubs, barking and growling. Then, Nell heard a sharp sound of pain and nothing else. Oh, no, something hurt Moonshine!

Nell scooted as fast as possible along the track. "Moonshine!" As she, too, entered the green glade, arms grabbed her like tentacles, and then she was struck from the side by something hard and sharp. Before she could struggle, she felt herself spinning into a black void. "Moon—"

Water surrounded Nell. She thrashed, trying to swim her way out of it, trying to find her dog. Her arm struck a hard surface, and she woke herself up. She was wet, but not swimming. The darkness around her was complete, at first. She felt whatever she hit, rough wood, and identified it as a flat, heavy timber like those in the Gem mine. Where was she? She felt around some more, finding mud and rocks. She gathered herself to stand up and hit her head with a *thunk,* enough to knock her back down, but not out. Lifting her hand over her head, she could feel rocks and more mud. It felt like a tunnel. With her hands guarding her head, she was able to sit up. Only then, did she see a sliver of light some distance from her, as if a needle were poking into the space. At the same time, a strong smell of cordite or gunpowder met her nose, and there was a low ripping sound in her ears. Her hackles rose. Something was going to explode nearby! As soon as she thought it, she wrapped her arms around her head, twisted herself to lie face down in the watery mud next to the timber, and pulled her legs close to her trunk. A fleeting image of Moonshine flashed in her head and then *Boom! Kaboom! Boom! Boom!*

Thunder rolled through Nellie, and pressure flattened her even more into the mud. The wave pulled her breath out of her lungs and then released her. She gasped for air, trying not to suck in water, but she choked and coughed. When she could raise herself on her arms and turn around, she felt the ground settling and earth and rocks falling close to her feet, which she could no longer stretch out in front of her. The pinpoint of light was gone. The smell of sulfur and smoke was so strong, she knew it must be surrounding her, but the blackness almost suffocated her, or maybe it was the debris of the explosion. She was caged in mud, dirt, smoke, maybe wood. No light. How long would the air last?

Nell wanted to scream hysterically, but no one would hear her, except perhaps the people—the men—who had fired off dynamite or some other explosive. The silence after the loud booms filled her head. She called once, but no sound emerged, only the effort inside her head. She was deaf. The men must assume she was dead, and she probably would be if they thought she lived through the blast and came after her. The pounding of her heart threatened to burst from her chest. But why her? Few people knew she and the sheriff were investigating bootleggers, and even fewer knew they were digging into the mine disaster, although the local law knew about the latter. Calm down. Take deep breaths, even if the fumes might be dangerous. She held the driest part of her shirt over her mouth to filter out possible poisons.

As her heart slowed and her panic diminished, she realized there was more space than she first thought. More rocks tumbled around her, mostly below her feet. Nell swept her arms carefully to her sides and once again felt the wooden timber. Maybe that had protected her. She pushed at it and it moved slightly but fell back again. Her fingers groped down the length of the wood to what felt like a half-pointed end. Back they climbed to the end nearest her. It might have been a half timber, it was so short, not as tall as the timbers in the Gem mine. She decided to try and gouge a space in the rocks below her feet, assuming that was the direction out of the tunnel, even though it looked blackest there.

Wait, she thought. Think this through. There was some source of light, because she was beginning to make out the low ceiling, the rocks and mud around her. She was on an incline with her head higher than the rest of her body, or at least that was the sense she had of her place in the earth. Could she scoot higher? She placed her elbows behind her shoulders, lifted her body a fraction and scooted her bottom along the ground an inch, then two. The space above her head narrowed. She began to tremble with fear of being entombed. Stop! Another long breath. Two. The smell had definitely subsided. It was escaping to somewhere. Or would it just be absorbed by the water and mud? Escape. Keep that thought.

Nell found the timber again with her right hand. She crawled her left hand across her chest and grabbed the timber with both hands, then pushed down with all her might. The timber moved, fractionally, but it moved. She shoved again, using her elbows as leverage. This time, it almost slid out of her grip. The mountainside was steeper than she had realized. Or maybe the dynamite had loosened a near mud slide, and soon the whole hillside would give way, Nell with it. She scooted herself down the short distance she had managed to climb up with her bottom and feet, grabbed the timber again with her arms, and pushed. As blunt as the half point on the other end had felt, it still moved mud and rocks aside, slowly to be sure. The rocky shelf above her head stayed in place, as near as she could tell, but her clothes felt wetter and colder.

"Moonshine, are you down there?" This time, Nell heard herself. Her hearing must be returning, although a ringing continued in her ears. Her voice sounded hoarse and uneven. She waited. "Moonshine? Where are you?" His yelp of pain might have been the last sound she would ever hear of him. Tears filled her eyes and dripped toward her ears. It was her fault. Why could she never let well enough alone or, at least, try not to do so much alone. The men always had partners in the mine. Even the bootleggers didn't operate without help. There had been two men lugging their burden along the track outside. Rosy and Charlie often operated alone, but they were strong and brave. She risked too much, trying to prove herself, as what? A man? She didn't want to be a man. She wanted to be a strong woman, wise, with courage and spirit. She felt failure seep into her limbs, her trunk, her head.

Then she heard a faint scrabble against rocks and dirt. "Moonie? Are you there?" The sound stopped, then began again. It sounded a long way from her. "Moonie? Get Rosy. Get Charlie." The scraping started, stopped, started, and then stopped completely.

If only it were Moonshine and he heard her. Rosy would be in the mine, so her dog couldn't find him until late in the day. She couldn't think where Charlie might be. She thought he might be going out to the back country again to find bootlegging stills. Maybe Moonshine would find him before he left.

She and her dog had left the hotel early.

Nell lay back down. She couldn't wait for help. She had to help herself. After a while, she gathered up her strength again and pushed on the half timber. It wouldn't go anywhere, so she groped her hands to the bottom again and felt a large rock in the way. She wanted to give up. She couldn't give up. She took her feet and kicked at the rock. It moved, and at the same time the half timber moved four or five inches. Progress. She shoved again and then slipped herself down a little to stay even with the timber. It was such hard work. As wet as she was, she closed her eyes—for a moment—and wrapped her arms around her chest to warm herself, if she could. Her trembling continued. She didn't know if it was from the chill or fear or both.

Chapter Fourteen

The sheriff knocked on Nell's door and waited. He could hear nothing—no footsteps, no bark from Moonshine. She must have gone out again on a walk. He was not sure he approved of all her exploring in the town. Her story about the man who accosted her worried him, although he now realized it was probably the revenuer who stalked Charlie in the woods—Julius Weber with the cowboy boots. Nell hadn't mentioned those, but then he may have been dressed to look like a worker in the smelter.

Charlie decided to go to the café for breakfast. Nell might not need morning sustenance, but he did. He also hoped to run into the Croat miner again, let him know how helpful he had been about going down the mine. He seemed to have disappeared. Charlie had sent Nell to the local brothel to see if he was there. Turns out he was but left before she could talk to him. The sheriff was surprised and mystified by how much Nell had liked meeting the local madam, Mimi. He and Nellie had heard about the madam's reputation in the valley—she ran a clean shop, served booze, and brooked no nonsense. Maybe he should meet her, too.

After breakfast, Charlie pondered his next step. He knew Rosy was going down into the mine today and would not come out until the shift ended. He hoped Rosy was able to gather some information; any information would help at this point. They had come up against a wall of silence, it seemed, as to the perpetrator of the explosion. He was making more headway finding bootleggers. He decided to visit the local morgue and find out what he could about the dead bootlegger and the cause of his death to confirm what Matt Wooden had told him. The local police had probably investigated, but Charlie wanted as many first-hand facts as he could find.

As he stepped outside, Moonshine limped up to him, barking and adding his strange *arp* sound, the one he used when something troubled him. Charlie knelt. "What's wrong, Moonshine?" He stroked the dog's head and neck and came up with blood on his hands. "You're hurt!" He stood up, expecting Nellie to appear. She didn't. He felt all along the dog's pelt. Behind one ear, Charlie found an egg-shaped welt and more blood. "All right. Sit still. I need to see what this is." Moonie sat on his haunches and let the sheriff knead his fur. The dog flinched and pulled his head away once but did not stand up or back away. He barked again when Charlie stopped touching the bad spot. Then he stood and moved several paces down the road. When the sheriff stood still, Moonshine jumped back and took hold of Charlie's trousers with his teeth and pulled.

"Where is Nell? Was she hurt, too?" Charlie squatted again. He wanted to take the dog to a veterinarian, but the dog had other ideas, he was certain. "Wait. I will get my revolver, a walking stick, and a jacket." He walked back into the Callahan Hotel and soon reappeared with a small pack on his back. "Let's go, Moonshine. You lead."

They almost ran down the road to the river. Lead Creek. Charlie thought the worst at first, that Nell had fallen in. If so, it would be a miracle if she were alive. The river raged, and whitecaps had formed. The water was so close to the bottom of the bridge, he worried the structure might go at any time. Both he and Moonshine dashed across, Charlie relieved that the river was not the dog's target.

Moonshine paused to pant. *Arp, arp.* He stopped to lap up water from a puddle and then continued his track. Charlie followed. The going was muddy and slippery. He had to knock mud from the bottom of his boots with the walking stick or a nearby stone, slowing his progress. Eventually, Moonshine ran so far ahead, Charlie lost track of him. He climbed, slipping here and there, hoping not to slide down into the river himself.

A ridge sloped down to the water's edge. The path around it exposed the sheriff to some risk of falling, so he grabbed a syringa branch. It was broken. Nell must have come along here, too. What in the world had she been doing? Ahead, he saw Moonshine disappear into a tangle of shrubs and brush. A rock slide ended in the greenery. "Moonshine, wait!" The dog reappeared and sat on his haunches until the sheriff caught up with him.

By now, the sun had moved higher in the sky, and steam floated from the ground. The sheriff noted the rocks were tailings from above. He moved into the glen and stopped. A huge pile of rocks and mud blocked his way. The dog climbed across the steaming stack, moving higher, beginning to bark. Charlie tried to follow, but the mess was slippery, and his boots sank into it as far as his ankles. The stick he carried helped steady him, but he was afraid of getting stuck or sinking up to his knees or more.

Moonshine pawed his way back and tried to urge Charlie forward. He barked and *arp*ed, looking up to what looked like the top of the stack. Charlie sniffed, recognizing the remnants of the smell. Dynamite, like in the mine. Someone had set it off, but who? And why? Nellie must be up there someplace. He planted one foot, used his stick, and planted another, sinking, but not as deep as his first few steps. "Nell!" Moonshine barked again. If she was buried in this mud, she could not have survived. Fear moved him faster and farther up the rockfall. Moonshine leaped forward, barking.

Nell woke herself up. She couldn't fall into a deep sleep. She would never awaken. Her chill remained, but not so cold, she decided. That must mean the sun was getting higher, warming the hillside. She decided she must aim the timber higher. Otherwise, she would just dig herself under the mud and rocks. She wanted to dig sideways, to get to the side of the exploded detritus. It seemed an impossibility, but, when she shoved the half-pointed end of the timber with her feet toward her right side, it moved—not easily, but it did move. She leaned forward, found the rock she had shifted earlier, and wedged it under the wood, to force the end higher. Again, she wound her arms around the top and shoved with all her might. The mud wasn't packed into such a dense wall, and her awkward shovel edged farther than any previous effort. She scooted forward and sideways and shoved again. As if she had signaled her dog, his barks greeted her movements. He was so much closer than the earlier scrabbling, before he left her alone. "Moonshine!" This time, she used all her effort to make her cry sound louder and longer. The answering cry, not a bark but a man's voice, brought tears out again. Moonshine had brought someone with him.

The possibility of being saved gave her greater strength, and she pushed the half timber again and again, making less progress and causing her to gasp for breath. "I'm here!" she shouted, and then she lost any power to make herself heard. She stopped shoving, hoping to hear the man's voice again, to hear Moonshine bark. Nothing. She sobbed, her shoulders shaking, her arms too tired to move, her body aching from cold and fright. Charlie, she thought. Help me.

After what seemed like an hour or more but might have been a minute or ten, sounds of metal scraping against rock and dirt reached her. So did *arp, arp.* Moonshine was back. So was help. Once again, she tried to angle her own wood piece to the right, to what she hoped was the edge of the rock and dirt pile. It moved so slowly, she stopped, hoping the metal equipment wielded by someone outside would make more progress. Then a shower of rocks fell on her and the timber. "Stop! Stop! You'll bury me!"

The sounds did stop. Nell needed protection, but what? She felt again along the timber. It was the only thing she had, so she pulled and pushed until she lay under it, her arms uncovered and still vulnerable, stretched out as if in a coffin. Terrible thought. "All right. Dig!"

"Nell? Can you hear me?" The sheriff's voice was as welcome as Moonshine's barks. The shoveling sounds grew closer, but nearer her feet than the rest of her.

"Charlie! Thank heavens!" Nell's voice sounded weak, even to herself. "I'm here. I can hear you. Be careful!"

And then a stream of light opened to the outside near the bottom of the half timber. "I'm here! I'm here! Help me! Oh, Charlie!"

"I can't see you! Wiggle something!"

Nell managed to kick one foot to the edge of the timber. "Here's my foot!" She could hardly speak for the sobs choking her. "Pull on me! I'm under a timber." She tried to extend her leg, but mud kept her pinned fast. "Be careful. Don't let the rocks bury me again!" She grabbed the wood one more time and pushed, like raising the lid of a coffin. She slipped out right into the sheriff's hands. He pulled her to him, surrounding her with his arms, his body, his warm heart.

Charlie Azgo held Nell for a while. She was only half conscious. He had to get her to a warm place, a hot bath. Taking her to the hospital would take too long. She might not survive the wait.

He stood up with her held in his arms. "Come on, Moonshine. We need to get Nellie warm and safe." He backtracked along the river path, across the bridge. Pieces of mud and rock fell from Nell as they hurried up the hill from the bridge. People cast him strange looks as they passed by on the road, skirting him with a wide berth so as not to get dirty themselves.

At the hotel, Charlie took the elevator to their floor. He hurried along to the bathroom at the end of the hall. No one was in it, so he laid Nellie on the bath rug and turned on the hot water spigot. Too warm, he thought. She needed heat but not too much. He added cold. Moonshine sat down near Nell and licked her face. She moaned.

Now for her clothes. The sheriff pulled off her boots and pants, full of mud. Her legs were stark white, especially in comparison to her shirt and jacket, also muddy. He managed to hold her against him and ease off those items of clothing until she was down to her underwear. Even they were soiled with mud. He told himself, he was the sheriff. This was just another body to handle and warm. Someone knocked on the door.

"Stay out." His voice shook a little. "We will be a while. Find another bathroom."

Steps moved away. Charlie lifted Nell up and placed her in the bathtub in warm water. As she warmed, he added more hot water. "Stay here, Moonshine. I have to get her robe and blankets." He peeked out. No one in sight. He hurried down the hall to her room. It was locked. "Damn." He dashed to his own room, retrieved his bathrobe and a blanket, and returned to Nellie. She was rousing.

"Can you stand? I will wrap this robe around you." He wanted to help her but thought she would not want to feel his hands on her.

Nell nodded but didn't move. "All right," Charlie said. He lifted her under her shoulders and she sagged against him. He wrapped the robe around her and laid her on the blanket he had spread on the floor. Where was her key? He looked in her jacket pocket and then her pants, spreading mud around the bathroom floor. He found it.

After he situated Nellie in her own bed, he dropped into the chair nearby. He could hardly not think of her pink and white legs and torso, her soft bottom, her silky hair, which he had washed of dirt before he lifted her out of the tub. She is only a body, he told himself. He fell asleep.

The sound of Nell murmuring awoke him, and he opened his eyes. "You are awake, Nell." He heaved a sigh of relief. "I did not know whether to take you to the hospital or try to warm you up here at the hotel. As you can see, I brought you here."

"How did I get in bed?" Nell tried to sit up. "I remember you pulling me out of the dirt." Her hand patted Moonshine, and she slipped back down. "He's hurt."

"I carried you across the bridge and up the hill," Charlie said. He motioned to Moonshine. "We found the bathroom down the hall empty and filled the tub with warm water. I put you in."

Nellie's face turned pink. "Wasn't I a little heavy? That is quite a ways to carry me."

"I think people who passed me by thought I was carrying a sack of mud and did not want anything to do with me." He smiled at her. "And pretty much, that was what I was doing." He cleared his throat and moved the chair closer to her bedside. "Tell me what happened."

"Did anyone help you?" Her voice had dropped again to a whisper.

"No. I have dealt with a number of bodies as sheriff. I hoped you would survive being cold for so long. And you have." He patted her shoulder. "Can you remember how you got buried?"

"Yes. No. Let me think." Moonshine hopped up on the bed

next to her. The sheriff moved to shove him off, and she stopped him. The dog crept up to lie between her and the sheriff. "No, let him lie. I was walking him along the river and saw two men on the other side. They acted so strange, I decided to cross the bridge and follow them. They disappeared around a bend. Moonshine and I kept going because it was such a lovely morning. Moonie ran into a bunch of shrubs after an animal, I thought. I followed him. Next thing I knew I was lying in a tunnel." She began to shake. Her dog barked his *arp*s, two of them.

Charlie leaned over Nellie and stroked her head. "You are safe, Nell. You are with me and Moonshine."

She closed her eyes and for a moment said nothing. "I found a timber beside me, like the ones in the Gem mine, only shorter. I tried to get up, but the tunnel was narrow, and I hit my head. Oh, someone hit me when I chased after Moonie. I didn't see anyone, though. Maybe I ran into a tree." She felt her head. A goose egg on her temple.

"There was blood on your cheek, when I pulled you from the mud. I doubt it was a tree limb. There were few trees around that steep hillside, only shrubs, although some of them were thick and tall." He stopped stroking her hair. "Did you recognize the men? And what was strange about them?"

Moonshine fell asleep next to her. "I don't know." Nell's eyes closed, then opened slowly. "I didn't recognize them. They were clear across the river. They carried a heavy load between them." She thought some more. "One of them kept looking behind them, as if they were afraid of being followed. That was my thought, so that was why I decided to follow them."

Charlie shook his head. "I think you need a full-time keeper."

"Are you volunteering?" Nell asked and then blushed again. Her eyes closed and stayed shut. She whispered something, and Charlie leaned close to hear. "Moonshine has the job already."

Chapter Fifteen

When Nellie awoke, she was in her room, her nightgown on, and Moonshine asleep in the chair by the bed, most recently occupied by Charlie Azgo. She lay quietly for a while, savoring the safety of the bed, the room, her dog, the warmth. Getting up and donning clothes seemed much too difficult, because it meant facing the problems and mysteries uncovered or still hidden in this mining area. She determined not to think about her recent rescue or being trapped in the mud. She wondered what time it was. She watched the shadow from the window and decided it was mid-afternoon. She must have slept for four or five hours. Too late to do much, although printing some of the negatives from her first trip into the mine might be possible. As Nellie dithered, she saw an envelope slip under her door.

With a huge sigh, she slipped out of bed and grabbed the bathrobe at the foot of the bed. It was Charlie's bathrobe, much too large for her. Still, she tied the sash until the robe almost doubled around her and smiled to herself. The envelope appeared to be from the front desk. Inside were two notes, one from Charlie and one from Ira, the miner from the hospital.

Charlie's: *Nell, do you feel well enough to accompany me to the Basque boardinghouse for dinner this evening? If so, please meet me in the lobby at 5:00 p.m.*

Ira's: *Miss Burns, I remembered more information. Could we talk? Meet me for breakfast tomorrow in the café next to the hotel. Ira Maki.*

"Well, Moonshine, I think our schedule is set for this evening and tomorrow morning. Would you like to go with me to the Hope Studio?" Nell felt up to moving, finally, and getting outside. Her whole body ached. She knew she had to move, to get her muscles going again. Otherwise, she would stiffen up like a board.

With her camera pack on her back and Moonie on a leash, Nell made her way down the street to see if she could use the Hope studio. Her muscles strained, but the walk helped stretch some of them. She knew the owner worked in the darkroom in the morning so might permit her to print the negatives this afternoon, even if she was later than she had scheduled. Indeed, this was the case. Moonshine rested in his front window, a circumstance that drew in several people, one of whom made an appointment for a portrait.

"You can leave him with me anytime, Miss Burns. He's like a magnet to people walking by. Last time he was here, he stayed by my side. Now, he seems to like the window."

"Thank you for the use of the darkroom," Nell said as she shook Mr. Hope's hand. "I'll remember about Moonie and might call on you again to keep him for a few hours, if needed." She took Moonie's leash in hand and limped back to the hotel with her prints. Leaning over the negatives in the developing trays hadn't helped her aches. She definitely wanted to go to the boardinghouse with Charlie. Both Mikel, Charlie's Basque acquaintance from sheep country, and Txomin might have learned more information about the mine explosion or about the bootlegging. The gossip around the table could prove informative. She thought that was what Charlie had in mind. Or perhaps he knew more, too.

The sheriff and Nell arrived as dinner was being served by Lorea—another "groaning board" of food, this time ham, potatoes au gratin, green beans, applesauce, olives, pickles, mustard, sausages, biscuits, green Jell-o and more, followed by bread pudding filled with raisins and cinnamon. Dominic, Lorea's husband, sat at the head of the table and made sure all the dishes passed around to the two guests more than once. It was the first meal Nellie had eaten all day, but she found she wasn't hungry. When most of the men had finished, they retired to the *mus* tables. Mikel, Txomin, Lorea, and Dominic stayed at the table with Charlie and Nell.

"So far, we have learned that most of the soft-drink parlors in Mullan and Wallace, at least, offer bootleg liquor for sale. These sales are permitted by license from the towns. Each parlor pays for their licenses—twenty-five to fifty dollars each, depending on the size of the parlor. The—uh—brothels"—Charlie glanced quickly at Nell—"pay the higher range, I understand, because there are more instances of calls for police help, or rather circumstances requiring police to break up fights, pick up drunks, and so on." The sheriff paused and looked at each of the others. "Any comments?"

Dominic, his voice as deep as a cello, said, "That fits. The city council here in Mullan approved the fine-by-license scheme. Someone decided they needed a legal opinion. That was a mistake because the opinion told them it was illegal. The mayor tried to shut it down, but the council overrode him." He laughed, his belly shaking, ashes from his cigarette dropping onto the tablecloth. The beard on the lower part of his jaw trembled, too. Unlike some of the men in the towns, Nellie observed, his beard was neatly trimmed and clean of any crumbs from eating. "The mayor quit, and the next one didn't make a fuss. So, the moonshiners kept their business. The miners kept their drink. The brothels kept their customers. And everyone is happy except the revenuers."

"I think the law is also involved," Charlie said. He nodded

toward Txomin. "Txomin here tells me some of the money goes to the police."

"That's one of the strange things about this whole situation," Dominic said. "None of the money goes into the city fathers' pockets or the law's pockets. It all goes to the town—half to the schools and half to the general fund. It may be illegal, but it ain't corrupt." He brushed the ashes off the table, stealing a look at his wife. She was busy stacking dishes.

"The town's budget isn't enough to cover town expenses," Lorea added. "They needed to do something after the Prohibition came in. Otherwise, the town would go bankrupt, and we wouldn't have no police help at all." Indignation marked her statement as her voice rose at the end. "What was the town supposed to do?" She shook her head. "The prohibitionists don't understand what it's like inside a mine or how hard these men work. They need their entertainment and drink." She carried a load of dishes through the door to the kitchen, *tsk*ing all the way.

The two Basque men stayed silent, drinking their hard cider. Nellie chuckled to herself. It seemed no one at the boardinghouse considered the hard cider to be "liquor." Even she had become used to the scorching element of the liquid. Tiny sips helped her swallow it, and she did feel more relaxed and less achy. She noticed Charlie did not partake but ignored the others' use. Her eyes wanted to close, but she forced them to stay open. Closed reminded her of the darkness in her mud cage.

"Have you heard anything in the mine?" Charlie asked. Txomin worked in the Gem mine, while Mikal labored in the Morning Mine there in Mullan. The switch in subject gave them a chance to participate if they desired.

Txomin lifted his chest, preparatory to speaking. He seemed happy to oblige. "Well between the jibber-jabber about union and non-union miners and a Pinkerton man at every shift when the men go down and then come out, nobody says much of anything. Down in the stopes, though, there's some thoughts. Rumor is two men were involved in the explosion—one a company man, a supe maybe, and the other a miner who has a grudge about something to do with the Gem. Probably both have a grudge against the company."

"Any guesses as to why?" Charlie leaned forward as if to catch all Txomin's words. He glanced toward Mikel, who said nothing, but he and Txomin exchanged looks.

Nell wondered if Txomin was talking out of turn. She wanted to ask who started or circulated the rumor, but she, too, said nothing, not wanting to divert him.

The tall Gem miner shook his head. "No idea. 'Course there's always some grudges going around—poor pay, bad hours, miners' con, shift changes, shortages on the measurements of lead mined. Who knows?"

"It must be some grudge, though." Nell finally inserted herself. "Six men dead, another dozen or so injured and some seriously." She wanted to bring up the dynamiting of the cave along the river that trapped her, but Charlie had cautioned her not to do so. He thought she might still be in danger if word got around that she had survived that blast. Miners loved to gossip, he insisted, and anything might be grist for their speculation and rumors.

"Some miners think that explosion was meant for one of the pickle barrels coming down," Mikel said, finally joining the conversation. "It went off too late and caught the men coming off shift. It was supposed to jam up the shaft, stop all work for anywhere from a few days to a few weeks, maybe even trap men underground. Definitely a big grudge."

"Maybe part of the union versus non-union battle?" Charlie asked. Nell nodded.

"Not quite like destroying the mill in '99, but coulda caused a lot of damage," Dominic said. "The company just shrugs at hurt miners. There's always more where they come from."

Nellie wondered at the poor opinion of the company. From what she'd seen at the hoist station, the managers who helped the hurt miners had taken extraordinary care to get them to safety, bind up wounds, hurry them to help. Maybe there was always a schism between workers and management. That was definitely true in the meat-packing plants in Chicago, she knew. Her own father had suffered the terrible work conditions there, before he became such a drunk and quit working. She wondered what her mother would say about all this. Were things in the West the same as those in the East? She suspected the Western Federation of Miners union would say yes.

"Nell, would you bring out those prints? It would help if we had names for all of the miners that were brought up. Not everyone ended up in the hospital, as near as I can tell, including you, Txomin."

The prints were in a side pocket of her pack. She brought them out—four of them, reflecting the four sleds she had photographed as they came into the hoist room. She had enlarged each to 8x10, to make the miners as identifiable as possible. Still, hastily wrapped bandanas and bandages and the iffy light didn't help with the identification of the men.

"Where were you, Txomin?" Nell asked. She wasn't sure she pronounced his name correctly. He almost preened to be back in the spotlight.

"I work days, so I was on the pickle barrel comin' to work. Because I was going deep, I was near the top of the sled." His head was no longer bandaged, and his arm had only a sling around it and his neck. "I managed to get on one of the sleds going up right away." He shuffled the pictures. "I might be in one of them."

"Then you might have been on the intended target if, as Mikel says, the blast was supposed to get incoming men on a sled," Nell said. "Is that right?" She glanced at both men.

"Well, yeah, I guess, if that rumor is right. But I don't know that it is. I'm more partial to the explosion being timed to get the muckers coming off shift." Txomin scratched his head. "But I coulda been, I guess. I'd taken the day off the day before. Maybe someone was mad at me."

"You was off spending your winnings from *mus*," Mikel said, laughing. "Tell her what you bought." His laugh turned into an extended chuckle.

"Ain't nobody's business what I bought," Txomin said, glaring at Mikel.

"He bought himself a new suit!" Mikel pounded the table. "He went all the way to Spokane to get it! He's courting a pretty missy up here, and he wanted to look handsome."

Lorea pushed through the door to re-enter the room. "Ah ha, I knew you were planning on courting Lillian." She patted his head as if he were a little boy. "Not sure a suit of clothes will be enough. She likes nice things." Lorea arched an eyebrow, picked up another stack of dishes, and left.

Chapter Sixteen

A watery sun shone through the thicker than usual smelter smoke as Nellie made her way outside the hotel the next morning. A good sleep, maybe from the hard cider, had eased many of her aches. She had left Moonshine sleeping on the bed. Charlie didn't seem to be up and about, so she made her own way to the café. She peeked through the front window. Only one person sat at the counter and no one at the tables. From the back, she couldn't tell if it was Ira, but she entered anyway and approached the man. He looked around and broke into a smile that spread across his face and twinkled his eyes.

"Ah, the photographer." Ira doffed his hat and placed it on the seat next to him on the farther side.

"Yes, Nell Burns, photographer. We met at the hospital." Nellie did a slight curtsy and smiled back. Ira looked so much better than he had in the hospital. His face was freshly shaved, his hair combed and only slightly mussed by his hat, a half-scrunched felt one. His shoulders were bent forward, as if he had spent a lifetime moving heavy loads. His dark face contrasted with his bare forearms that almost reflected the light, they were so pale. His wrapped hand still carried a plump bandage, but he no longer appeared to be in pain. "How is your hand? Have you been able to work?"

Ira lifted his injured hand. "They put me in the assay office. I been sorting samples and weighing rocks." He motioned for her to sit down. "Don't pay as much, but it keeps me busy until I can go back underground. The company found work for most of us who can manage one handed or one legged." He looked around and lowered his voice. "We could form our own crippled union," he said, chuckling.

"I'm surprised," Nellie said. "Most people—not miners, I mean—criticize the company and blame it for the explosion, one way or another."

"Nah, we're a company town. We may call the company names and moan and groan, but that's normal. On the whole, old Gem doesn't do so bad by most of us. The Butte mine is a whole lot worse. That's why so many Butte miners come here."

"I see," Nellie said, but mostly she didn't. Even Rosy, a true short-timer, had little good to say: broken equipment, ill-repaired hoses, missing drills and scalers, old and dangerous giant powder. He compared the Gem to the Triumph mine near Hailey and said that one was better kept up. Of course, he had said, it was much smaller.

"Are you married, Ira?"

"Nope. Ties a man down too much." He sipped his coffee and pushed away a platter filled only with remnants of a breakfast. "Can I order something for you?" He waved to a waitress who stood down the counter from the two of them. "Are you?"

"Am I what? Oh, married. No." She gave an order of scrambled eggs and bacon to the waitress and turned to Ira. "Why is this café so empty? Usually there are three or four tables of men." She glanced around and back at Ira. He seemed to be watching her, and she felt slightly uncomfortable.

"There's a meeting this morning before the shift starts up. The men are talking about a strike until the company comes clean."

"But I thought you said the company wasn't to blame—"

"No, I said the company mostly does right by us. That doesn't mean they don't make mistakes or mistrust one or another of us. Take Savich, for instance. He got fired because he didn't show up for work, sent someone else in his place, and that man got kilt in the explosion. Wasn't Izzie's fault."

"I heard that story. A man wouldn't have died if Izzie had showed up." Nell's food came, and she ate slowly, taking in Ira's various expressions when she could. She asked for a cup of tea and waited until it came before turning more his way.

"Maybe Izzie would have died. Probably would have. There's other stories. Bad ones are short-changing the men on their rock in the box—how far they get in a stope. Lots of rowls over that."

"Enough to cause a miner to try to close the mine?" Nellie studied her companion. His serious expression and comments worried her. She wondered if he had been short-changed. "Do you have any information for us?"

Again, Ira glanced around. The waitress had gone through a door to the kitchen. No one else entered the café. "I was told it was a joint effort between a company man and a powder monkey. One of the muckers had been blabbing about a rich find up the road, and the Gem wanted to keep that quiet. The powder man had been short-changed a couple times and wanted to get even. Don't know if this information is true or not. The mucker wasn't getting the medical care he needed, or so it was said. If a mucker knew about the rich find, so did everyone else on his shift." He shook his head "All miners and muckers are gossips, you know."

And maybe this was Ira's gossip, Nellie thought. "Where was the discovery, do you know?" Nellie had a premonition that it was where she had been buried. Someone wanted it undiscovered.

"Up the road a piece, on the way to Wallace, below the Monitor, which is open from time to time. Not much there. This new mine—but maybe a really old one—was re-discovered. Called the Crystal. I'd heard of it. No secret there." Ira shrugged his shoulders and slapped his leg with his good hand. "Could be a big fat story. Everybody and his dog has a secret 'rich find' in this valley."

"Ira, someone at the hospital mentioned a Crystal mine." Then she told him about her own narrow escape. "Any idea who might have wanted to close that tunnel?"

"Omigosh, Miss Burns. I'd heard there was a cave-in out of town. Were you hurt?"

"Mostly frightened almost to death." She touched his shoulder above the hurt hand. "I didn't get wounded like you did." She wondered how long she would have nightmares or before she'd be able to trust any miner in this town. She even thought Ira acted a little suspicious. He already knew she and the sheriff were investigating the explosion inside the mine. Maybe his hand was hurt when he set off dynamite inside, and he was throwing suspicion elsewhere when he said he was coming down the shaft.

"You were going to think on the man you saw heading down the drift after the explosion. Have you had any other thoughts?" Nellie sipped her tea and didn't look directly at Ira. He seemed to back away from her when she was too direct.

"Hmmm. He did seem kinda familiar. In the mine, you get used to seeing the men, how they walk and dress, carry themselves, so to speak. You don't look at them directly with your carbide lights, 'cause the light can blind 'em, so faces don't count so much as shape, kind of. Seems like the man I saw was limping, but there was something else, too. I can't seem to pull it out of my head." He shook his head, as if trying to loosen a thought.

That made sense to Nell and also explained why Ira didn't often look directly at her. It wasn't guilt. It was habit from being in the mine. She waited, but Ira didn't pursue his answer. "If you do think of what else made the man familiar, would you tell me?"

Ira nodded his head and patted around his chest until he found a pack of cigarettes. He pulled one out and lit it with a match from a matchbook. Nell caught a glimpse of the cover and thought it mentioned the name of one of the bars in Wallace—the St. Regis, one of the places where she and Charlie had visited. It was next door to a stairway that led up to a brothel. Ira had said he was single, but Nell didn't want to ask if he frequented any of those places. That truly seemed like none of her business. She couldn't think of other questions, and Ira began to get off the counter stool. "There might be lots of men who limp in the mine," Nell said. Still, Ira didn't add a guess or name. "Anything else I should know?" Nellie asked.

"Guess that's all I got for you, Miss Burns. Thanks for meeting me. I got to get to the assay office. I hope next time I see you, I'll be back on shift in the mine. My partner wants me back. He has a greenhorn who don't like the work." He lifted his bandaged hand. "I get this off in another couple days, I hope. Doc Parker says I can go back underground then."

"Ira, thank you for contacting me. If I wanted to get in touch with you, how would I do that?"

"Just ask at the boardinghouse back behind the green grocer's. Someone there will pass along a message, iffen you want."

Nell nodded and gathered her coat and camera pack. She waved at him as he left the café. A few men passed him on their way in—nobody she recognized. The meeting must be over.

Charlie or she was supposed to check out the shift records to see who was getting off work, who was coming down the man-sled, and who were the shifters and supervisors. Moonshine needed walking, and she wanted to be by herself for a while and think about what she had learned from Ira and the Basque men. Maybe she should find Charlie, though, and they could decide what to do next.

Charlie picked up a note from Nellie at the front desk of the hotel. She wanted to meet. He did, too, but he was not certain what their next steps should be. Against his express wishes, she had visited the Hope Studio before he thought she had recovered and printed out more photographs. He could go over those again with her. The Basque men had given them a couple of names, ones with which he wasn't familiar. Nell was good with ideas and had better eyes than he did. He had been wondering if he should get eyeglasses, because it seemed like he missed a lot when he did look at the photos, especially the negatives, although in part that had to do with deciphering white on black rather than black on white. He had a difficult time turning the images around in his mind.

The sheriff knocked on Nellie's door but received no answer. She was probably out with Moonshine. He knew she had met with Ira, the miner, early in the morning. He decided to go outside to find her, first checking in at the café. He ran into her at the hotel door, dog on leash and her camera on her back. Her mouth turned up on greeting him. He inspected her carefully before even saying anything. The bruises on her face appeared to be diminishing, and she stood as straight as always. "You seem in good spirits. How do you feel? Any residual aches or pains?"

"I'm still a little tired, Charlie. But on the whole, I don't feel as if I was under a ton of mud yesterday. Do I look like I was?"

"No, your bruises are not quite so black. They are green and yellow instead of raging purple." He lifted her chin with his folded fingers and studied her more closely, turning her face from side to side. "How about the rest of you?"

Nellie blushed and moved her chin away from him. "You might know better than I."

Charlie felt his own face get hot, so he turned around to open the door for her. "Let's go to that conference room and look over the prints of the miners again. Do you have them with you?" He followed her through into the hotel and then into the conference room. He wondered if anyone else ever used it. The hotel was singularly empty most of the time, although there was traffic that went up and down the one elevator in the evenings. He could hear the sound from his room.

Nellie laid the prints out along the table in the order taken. The black and white images were sterile compared to the scenes as Charlie remembered them. He had helped unload the men and get them situated in the trolleys taking the men outside to ambulances and other transportation to the hospital. Nell regarded them with what appeared to be a critical eye, lifting one and then another and tilting them one way or another to catch the best light.

"I can improve them, Charlie, but it seems to me that these reflect the men fairly well. Larger or more careful printing probably won't improve what we can see." She lowered each one and glanced at him. "I can recognize a couple of the men from my hospital visit. What do you think? And Mikel and Txomin gave us a few names. We could get one of the supers to identify the others for us. Then we could compare them to the shift records, which we still haven't studied, unless you have." She stepped back, giving him more room to assess what the prints reflected.

Charlie was always surprised at the detail Nellie's photos showed. He, too, picked up each print and held it close and then further away. "I think I am as much interested in who is not in the sleds as who is," he said and continued, "and who is helping or standing around. The whole situation seemed so chaotic."

"Yes, in some ways, I wish we had been at the accident scene itself. That must have been even more traumatic, but also more informative. Who wasn't hurt? And why not?" She selected the third one. "Mostly I focused on the sled itself, but, in this print, my focus picked up a couple of men greeting the sled as it came to a stop out of the shaft. Recognize anyone there?"

There were three men standing at the far side of the sled, two leaning toward the men in it and the third somewhat behind the others and closer to the camera. Charlie reached for the photo. "Yes, I think that is Buddy Rinaldi, a lead shifter, the one who took me around and explained the operations in the mine." He pointed to the nearer figure. "I'm not sure about the other two." He tilted the photo back and forth as well, squinting. "That one," he said and pointed, "might be Harry Pierce, a supervisor. He's the one who took us down to the scene. Kind of a hot head, I thought." Charlie had been called to the scene by the local police, which in itself was a little strange. Would all company personnel, meaning the supervisory level, have been called in at the same time? he wondered. Or were some of them already there? If so, and one or more of them had been at the accident, how fast would they have been able to reach Level Nine, the main level for getting inside and outside the mine? More questions to ponder. The shift records loomed as more important information than he had thought earlier. He wondered if those records would include Rinaldi and Pierce, as they did not seem to be hourly miners.

Nell again studied prints four and five. "This one has bystanders as well. Are they the same men? If so, we need to go over the shift records, don't you think?"

Charlie smiled inside. Nell was becoming an excellent detective. "Yes. I'll begin on those tomorrow if the mine office will give me access. I think it is time you went back to Mimi's house to take photographs. See what you can find out from the women. If anyone knows some of the secrets of the miners, they do."

Chapter Seventeen

The bordello owned by Mimi sat at the corner of Main Street and Railroad Avenue, not far from either the train station or the river. Even so, it was quiet when Nellie approached the front door. Once again, she wasn't certain whether to walk in or knock. The door opened before she could decide.

"We're expecting you, Miss Burns. The girls are all excited—and dressed up. They've all had police photos taken, but not nice ones." Vicki St. Clair ushered Nell through the double doors. She was an attractive woman, older than Nell would have imagined for a "woman of the night," but then, what would she know? Hailey had at least one "house," but she had never seen its occupants, only the occasional man going in and out through a red door. "Right through here. Mimi said to let you get set up in the private room. The light is good in there."

The room was much the same as when Nell visited earlier. She studied where the best light entered through windows. The light switch was black and white buttons, one above the other on a plate on the wall. "May I?" Nellie asked before she pushed the white button. Vicki nodded. A center chandelier leaped into light. Nell doubted if it was used very often, but it would serve well for portraits of the "girls."

"I'll check back," Vicki said.

"No, I need someone to pose in several places, so I can find the best, most flattering light. Please stay." Nellie unpacked her camera and tripod and set them up. Then she directed Vicki here and there. The woman struck poses—a sultry look, a side profile, a flirtatious expression, and several more. Both she and Nell laughed as Nell moved her around the room. Vicki was taller than Nell and heavier, but she had a graceful way of walking. They finally settled on a spot near the window, where the chandelier gave a sideways glow to the poseur. "All right, Miss St. Clair, I think I'm ready. Ask Mimi if she wants her photo taken. I already took a couple of you."

The first girl—what should she call them, Nell wondered to herself—came in, flouncing in an ankle-length, filmy dress that outlined her figure, a buxom silhouette for a side portrait. Nell took two photos of each woman—face and shoulders only and then full figure. She was using her filmback, the same kind of film she had used at 4th of July Lake in the Stanley Basin when she photographed the women tourists. Those photos had been quite successful in that every woman purchased one of herself. Most of them also purchased a photo of the cowboy leader of the campout. The conflict then between cowboys and sheepherders seemed more straightforward than the situation she and Charlie were facing here in the mining area. Moonshining complicated both assignments.

After each photo session ended, the girls stayed in the room and watched the others. They also gossiped. Nellie paid as much attention as she could to the conversations, but most were about clothes, hair, and nail polish, subjects not interesting to her. By the fifth girl, the back and forth had turned to the mining explosion, so her ears strived to catch what was being said. She slowed down her photographing process, the better to hear.

"Who do you think did it?" was how the talk started. The girls all seemed to know what the subject was. "I heard . . ." began most of the answers, mostly speculation as near as Nellie could determine. One was more specific: "Ira told me he saw someone in the tunnel running away from the shack that got dynamited. Said it looked like that supe he didn't much like—can't think of his name. He don't come here, as far as I know." Someone else declared, "Too cheap!" They all laughed.

"Why would a supervisor help torch the shack?"

"I don't know. Another way to blame the union. The company hates the union, just because the men want to earn an honest wage."

"Or even a dishonest wage," giggled another. "My best customer brings in drills, and I turn 'em back in to the company and get paid that way, sometimes." When Nellie turned to see who said that last statement, she met the eyes of one of the prettier of the girls, who blushed and looked away.

"One of my clients—he's a miner—said some of the supes take supplies and sell them."

"Where would they sell things and what kind of things?"

Nell couldn't see who was talking, as her head was back under the black cloth.

"I dunno. Maybe dynamite? Don't loggers use dynamite on roots and logs?"

"You see that Cadillac that one guy drives?"

A few more mumbles back and forth that Nell couldn't decipher. The talk turned to automobiles and fur coats, money, and dreams.

The "girls" weren't really girls. Several were in their twenties. A couple were much older. None of them would attract much attention on the street as being beauty queens. Dressed up, each had a kind of small-town girl appeal, or, in some instances, a country girl look—slightly plump and even healthy appearing. One or two were much too thin and verged on being jittery and sharp edged. They sat around in the comfortable club chairs, their legs slung over the arms, and chatted in a desultory manner. Each followed Nell's directions, shifting shoulders, smiling, looking down or up. When the last girl finished, number eight,

Mimi came in and shooed everyone out of the room.

"Do you want your photograph taken, Mimi?" The madam was probably one of the most beautiful women Nell had ever seen. She may have been over forty, but her skin glowed, her figure was straight and curvy at the same time, and her hair shone as if she brushed it hundreds of times every night. It was long, but rolled up in the latest fashion for long hair. Hers was as dark as Nellie's hair, but Nell felt her short-cropped hair looked unsophisticated next to Mimi's. Nell envied her presence, wishing she herself walked and talked with such confidence and stature. Maybe at forty she would, having earned it with her photography, her art. Her dream sounded as speculative as the girls' dreams about their futures—a house with a picket fence, a man with money and ease, a child or two or three.

"I'm too old, Miss Burns. There is no one to whom I could send a photograph, nor anyone I could give one to." She paused then, and a fleeting look of regret passed her face. "Would you like to meet someone special to me?"

"Yes, of course," Nell said, wondering why that "special" person wouldn't want a photograph of Mimi. "I am finished here, unless you change your mind." She smiled to let Mimi know she was not pushing.

Mimi left the room but within a few minutes returned, shepherding a small girl who had the same gray-green eyes as Mimi, and hair a lighter chestnut color in ringlets. Her heart-shaped face was a replica of Mimi's. "Hello," Nell said and held out her hand. The little girl put her hand in Nell's and curtsied with a small smile. A dimple creased one cheek.

"Say hello, Cassandra. This is Miss Burns. She is a professional photographer, an important woman in this state." To Nell, she said, "I am Cassandra's aunt." Her emphasis on the word "aunt" did not fool Nell. "Cassandra is four years old."

"Hello, Miss Burns." Cassandra's voice was almost a whisper.

"Hello, Cassandra. I am so pleased to meet you." Nell glanced at Mimi and motioned to her camera with a question on her face.

Mimi nodded. She knelt to the child and asked, "Do you want your photograph taken? It will be printed on a piece of paper and look just like you. You could give it to your Auntie Dolly."

Cassandra nodded and looked at Nellie. "Would you please take my picture, Miss Burns?"

"Indeed I will. You must promise to hold very still for me." She placed the child in the same place the women had posed and took two photos—a side profile and a front face, as she had for the others. "You did very well, Cassandra. I will have the prints for you in several days. Can you wait that long?"

The little girl nodded, then moved to Mimi, where she took the woman's hand and sidled close to her. "Thank you." Mimi took her out of the room and returned in a few moments.

"Mimi, one of the girls talked about the explosion in the mine, saying Ira, whom I have met, named a supervisor he didn't like as being one of the instigators. Do you think that is true?"

The madam thought a moment. "That could be Pierce. I suspect that whatever Ira told her was true to Ira. He rarely speculates. He could have made a mistake, however." She looked at her watch. "It is getting late, and I have errands to run, and I must get Cassandra back to her home. I can make some enquiries and perhaps pin down information that most people do not have." She stepped closer to Nell. "Thank you for being so sweet to Cassandra. She is my daughter, as you guessed, I can see. She doesn't know that, however."

"She will if she stands next to you and looks in a mirror," Nell suggested. "Especially as she gets older. She is a lovely child, Mimi."

Chapter Eighteen

Sheriff Azgo pulled down the ledger book for 1924 from the shelf in the mine's paymaster's office. Red leather bound the spine, and a pebbled, beige surface marked the cover of the heavy book. Opened, it was almost as wide as the top of the desk. Charlie had gained entry via the police chief's office after being refused by the paymaster, even after showing his sheriff's identification. Working after hours helped him concentrate on the details of the ledger pages, although he found himself taking more time than he expected figuring out all of the columns and notations. Again, his vision seemed to swim from time to time. He wished Nell were with him, but she and Rosy had decided to crash a union meeting, Nell in her male garments and armed with her camera.

Each page contained a couple dozen names, in order of hire, reflecting shift worked, changes to shifts, and pay amount. For miners, there were notations about "rock in the box," which he assumed meant number of cars filled from particular named or numbered stopes. A pound mark seemed to mean the mining ended at a stope, although he noticed sometimes notations continued after another name. Maybe it meant the miner left or changed jobs. Or died.

Harry Pierce's name appeared nowhere. As a supervisor he was probably paid by the month or was in a different list. Rinaldi did appear, so was paid by the shift, but at a higher rate than most miners. He worked the day shift the morning of the explosion but must not have left the hoist room before the explosion so was able to help with the injured men.

Charlie looked for Rosy's name and found it. His notations were limited because he had only worked a couple of days and had not yet been paid. He looked for and found Savich, whose notations included the day of the explosion, even though the man said he had not worked that day, that someone else had taken his place and died as a result. A mark ended that row. The sheriff did not know the replacement's name. Still, it was worth checking with the supervisor, whose initials marked the head of another column. He wondered if Izzie got the money or the paymaster did.

The explosion had occurred as the graveyard shift of muckers ended and the day shift of miners and timberers was arriving. Charlie found the correct date and time and began noting names of those going off shift. The paymaster, or someone, maybe the super, noted those killed or injured in the row where notations stopped. He followed the dates and found a few injured men began work again, not necessarily underground. Ira, whose last name was Maki, showed up as working in the assay office. Txomin was gone the day before the explosion, as he had described.

The pay amounts fluctuated, reflecting deductions for money owed to Gem, maybe for company store purchases, tools, supplies. Charlie could not determine all of the deductions from the notations, only that there were a lot. He would check with a company official to be sure all such deductions were appropriate. He made a note to do so. Maybe the paymaster was cheating.

Late in the evening, Charlie had amassed several pages of notes. He folded the pages into thirds and placed them inside his jacket in a pocket. As he left the office, he realized no one else was in the building, a one-story affair almost a block long.

A walkway extended across the front with doors to each office breaking up the expanse. A light shone at each end, but none in the middle. He closed and locked the door and began walking to the east end, the nearest to the mine entrance up the way. A shot rang out, and a wood board above his head splintered. Charlie ducked as low as he could and jumped down from the walkway. Two more shots blasted from the dark street area, both missing him, maybe on purpose. He had been a good target against the whitewashed building until he scooted down and off the ramp.

A shadowed niche gave Charlie some protection. He hid as much of his body as he could and waited. Eventually, he heard running steps, an automobile starting up and then speeding in the direction toward the smelter and away from town. It was the only auto on the road. He waited a while longer and then stretched himself up and out of the niche. He hurried around the corner of the building and eased his face out to search the grounds around him. No more shots. He had walked from the hotel to the mine offices, so he scurried in shadows along other outbuildings and shacks until he was on the road leading back uptown. A few streetlights marked his way, but he stayed outside the pools of light. Soon, the late afternoon shift of workers would be coming out of the mine, and the graveyard shift would line up to enter. The super had told Charlie that the graveyard shift was mostly muckers, timberers, and diggers—no powdermen—and that shift was much smaller than the earlier shifts. He explained what each of the job descriptions meant: muckers cleaned out ore and debris not finished by the afternoon shift, shoving everything down chutes. On the day shift, the skip tenders released all the ore from the chutes into ore cars to be transported out to the rock crusher, mill, and smelter. Diggers worked on repairing chutes and digging more, using shovels. Timberers built the square sets to hold the headwalls up. Digging was the hardest work of all, although the skip tenders suffered more injuries than most of the other jobs because of ore and rocks getting stuck in the chutes. Second most-frequent injuries were from rock bursts and air blasts when miners were caught and buried by the mountain. Charlie could not fathom working in a mine. He would rather go back to sheep herding than be stuck underground for even a day.

Nell stood so much shorter than Rosy that she was sure the miners at the union meeting would know she was a woman. Her miner's cap covered her hair. She wore pants and boots, and she had smeared her face with dirty water from one of the puddles along the road as they walked from the hotel down to the nondescript building being used by the miners for union meetings. The Gem Company knew they were there, Rosy said, and the miners knew they knew. So far, no one had tried to break up the meetings, but there were always rumors of spies and then men laid off from the mine. Other mine owners and companies up the valley weren't so picky about union membership, although none of the companies was happy about the demands made for more money and safety changes.

At the door, Rosy showed his work card, said he was new and had brought a friend along, gesturing to Nell, who tried to stay mostly behind him. She kept her head low. Rosy said, when questioned, that Mike had invited him. That seemed okay with the door guard, and they were admitted. The room contained maybe twenty or so men, some sitting in scattered wood chairs, but most standing in groups of two or three. One of the bushier bearded miners called out to Ross, Rosy's real name, and he and Nell sauntered over.

"This here is my pard, Ned Cord," Rosy said. "He just arrived from south Idaho and was thinking of getting on at the

Gem. We both worked in the Triumph mine down there at one time."

Nell nodded her head, again keeping her eyes downcast. She wished she had a brimmed hat instead of the knit one. She grunted, as if to say hello. Rosy turned from her and began talking to the men around them. "Will I get fired because I came to this here meetin'?" He took off his hat and shook his head. "I shore do need the money and hate to take the chance."

"We all gotta take the risk," his bushy bearded friend said. Nell hadn't caught his name. "Otherwise, we ain't never gonna get a raise from these here cheapskates. Nothing ventured, nothing gained, I say."

Nods and grunts answered him. "We got to get enough men to strike, or we ain't never going to get anything at all."

"They're calling us Bolshies already. I'm a true blue American," one man said. Others murmured agreement.

A man on a raised dais at the front of the room called for order. "You all know why we are here. We need more recruits. I see Ross brought a new man, short as he is. Anyone else?"

Nellie felt everyone staring at her. She was sure she blushed from the deception, if nothing else. Rosy raised his arm and gestured to her. Then he turned and faced the speaker. "If I'm the new guy and no one else brought anyone, how are you gonna get enough men to strike?"

That turned the attention back to the front of the room. "Men are afraid to come out. They got families and can't afford to get fired. There are lots more with us. We just need to get organized."

Whatever that means, Nell thought. She didn't blame anyone for not showing up. The mine explosion probably scared the men, too. Especially if it was the company that was responsible. She hoped she and the sheriff could find the culprit. Maybe Charlie would turn up something in his record search. She wished she were with him and not here. She didn't see any opportunity to take photographs without disturbing the men and being accused of spying for the Gem Company. Then she spotted the man who had accosted her outside the boardinghouse—a smelter man he had called himself. From what Charlie had said, he wasn't connected with the mine operation at all—he was a revenuer. She shifted so she could see his feet. Yes, cowboy boots. What was he doing there? Nell turned her back, so he wouldn't see her face. The pack on her back became a telltale sign of who she was.

"Rosy, I think we need to go. I recognized someone here, and he may recognize me," Nell whispered to Rosy's back. He looked around and then moved closer to her.

"Yeah, this wasn't such a bright idea."

The door slammed open, and four men with revolvers shouted and crowded into the room. "Stand still, all of you. We have you covered. This here meeting is illegal. No unions are allowed in this valley!" This man, whose face was covered with a bandana from his nose down, gestured to someone behind him.

Rosy moved in front of Nell, and she cowered behind him.

The man who came forward wore a suit and tie and carried a tablet. "I'm taking names, and you can all consider yourselves fired from the Gem." His face was not covered, but Nell didn't recognize him. She wondered if the men in the room did. The name-taker wore glasses and a city hat. He began to pace, and Nell noticed his feet. His shoes looked as if he had walked through mud, they were so cracked-looking.

Several of the miners had moved to one end of the room, and one man smashed a window and jumped to get out. A second man succeeded and escaped as well, but the third man was caught by one of the armed intruders, who pulled him toward the front door and shoved him out into the night.

Nell whispered to Rosy, "Keep standing in front of me. I am

going to get my camera out and try to take a photograph of these men. Meetings are not illegal. What they are doing is."

Rosy pulled his bearded friend close so they formed a shield in front of Nellie. When another two men saw what she was doing, they gathered close to Rosy and his friend. Another man across the room began shouting at the intruders and the man with the tablet. "You can't stop us from meeting. I know my rights. Get out of here."

One of the intruders raised his revolver and shot into the air. The noise was deafening inside the room. "This here gun says we can stop you and fire you. Get up here and give us your name."

The angry man stomped to the front of the room and shouted out, "Charlie Chaplin." Then he slammed out the door. Slowly, one man and then another lined up. Each shouted out a famous name: Douglas Fairbanks, Valentino. The scribe in the suit realized almost immediately that no correct name was being given. He gestured to one of the masked men. "Hold your gun next to his head. Maybe we'll get serious here."

Nellie had fumbled getting her camera out and the bellows pulled open. She had brought another roll film camera back. Still, she would have to balance the Premo on something firm, as she had not brought her tripod. And the subjects of her photographs would also have to hold still. She wouldn't be able to squat down to focus using the wire viewer on the camera top, so she would have to guess on where the bellows should be and try to aim the wire toward her subjects—the men in front. "I'm not sure this will work, Rosy. When I say 'kneel,' do so, and I'll place my camera on your head. Someone else will have to shout something to keep the intruders occupied in one place for as long as possible. Any ideas?"

Rosy conferred with his companion, who nodded. This group still stood toward the back of the room and so far had not drawn the attention of the armed men and the suited scribe. "All right, Missy. We're ready."

"Kneel," Nell said.

Rosy's friend shouted, "Damn you all to hell! I got a gun, and I'll kill all of you!" It had the desired effect. All heads turned to Rosy's group. Nell placed her camera on Rosy's head when he knelt and took three photographs in as rapid succession as she thought would still give her definition and not just blurs. Then she removed the filmback and slipped it inside Rosy's jacket as he stood up again.

The scribe dashed up to Nellie and grabbed her camera. She didn't want it to break so she released it to his grasping hand. "Careful. It is a delicate instrument!"

"Gimme the film!" He held the camera high. "Or I'll drop it!"

"It's in the camera!" she screamed. "Give it back, and I'll give you the film."

He stared at her a moment. Everyone in the room stood still, and no one said a word, either from shock that Nell was a woman or that she had taken photographs. Bushy beard took a short, dark object from his pocket and knocked the scribe on his head. He fell over. Then a melee broke out among the union men and the intruders. A miner grabbed the camera and passed it to another man as one of the armed men made a grab for it. The revenuer snatched it, hurried to the window, and dropped it outside.

"Oh, no!" Nell cried. "Rosy, run out and see if you can save it! My camera!"

He dashed to the door, shoved a masked man aside, and hurried out the door. Nellie was too small to shove anyone, but she managed to scoot around the melee and join Rosy outside, only he had disappeared. Nell ran around the corner. There, Rosy grappled with yet another masked man who had Nell's camera in hand. The bellows looked as if they had twisted and were broken.

Anger flooded Nell, and she leaped on the back of the thief, pounding at his arms. "Let go!" she shouted. A large man, he shrugged hard, and she flew to the ground, where she grabbed his leg and twisted. He screamed and dropped the camera. Rosy scooped it up, grabbed Nellie's arm, and pulled her up and along with him as he hurried away from the union building.

"Sorry I got you into this, Nellie."

"Do you still have the film?" Nellie's voice was ragged as she limped and tried to keep up. She reached for the camera. "Let's get somewhere I can figure how much damage was done." She was still so angry that she wasn't sure if the tears spilling down her cheek were from rage or for her Premo. It practically hung from Rosy's hand, although he tried to cradle it in his arm. Rosy let go of her arm and put his around Nellie's shoulders. They stopped in an alley near the YMCA, and Rosy helped steady Nellie while she tried to close up the bellows. Part of the material was torn, and she couldn't fold the bellows into the camera box. One of the wood panels hung down like a broken wing.

"Oh, dear. What am I going to do without my camera?" What a disaster, she thought. Why didn't she go with Charlie? "I'll have to see what I can do to repair it back at the hotel. You keep the film until we get there, just in case."

Two shots rang out. "Oh no. I hope no one is hurt!" She wanted to head back and see what was happening, but Rosy held onto her shoulders.

"We're going to the hotel. Nothing but trouble back there. We'll act like we came from dinner. All the folderol had nothing to do with us."

Nellie wanted to cry but held her anguish in check. "I'm so glad we didn't bring Moonshine with us. He might have been killed by one of those men."

"Where's the sheriff? We coulda used him." Rosy's steps were twice as long as Nellie's, and she had to hurry to keep up with him.

"He's at the mine office, researching the shift records. I hope he found some good information." Nell now had the Premo camera cradled in both her arms, her own wounded child.

CHAPTER NINETEEN

The sheriff and Rosy and Nell converged at the hotel door. There was a collective sigh of relief that all of them appeared safe and sound.

"Did you hear those shots?" Charlie asked.

"Yes," both Rosy and Nell answered. "Armed men who broke into the union meeting," Nell added. "One man shot into the ceiling, and we heard the others after we left."

"Someone shot at me as I left the paymaster's office. I thought whoever fired those returned to finish the job." He opened the door. "What's wrong with your camera, Nell? Did you get some photographs at the union meeting?"

"It's a long story," Nell said. She wanted to cry in her beard, but she didn't have one. "Can we get something to eat? Rosy and I'll tell you what happened. Then you can tell us who tried to shoot you."

"Danged place," Rosy said. "Let's go home and let all these men shoot each other. I'll take my piddling Triumph mine in central Idaho any day."

Nellie brought Moonshine down, and the three of them found an open café with few people in it. They sat at a back table with the sheriff facing the front door. Moonie sat next to Nellie. She felt as if he were protecting her from anyone who came through the door, and she checked to see if there was a back way out. She had left her damaged camera in her room wrapped in a blanket on her bed before locking the door.

Rosy had already jumped in and described the union leader, the masked intruders, the unmasked scribe taking names—all false names as near as he could tell—and then the melee. He turned to Nellie. "You can tell about your camera and my head." He chuckled and rubbed the top of his thinning hair. "Makes a pretty good tripod if I do say so myself."

Nellie finally felt herself calming down, even thinking she could get her camera repaired at the Hope Studio. She squeezed Rosy's arm. "Thank heavens you were with me. Of course, I couldn't have gone in alone anyway, but . . ." she said and turned to Charlie, "he made a good screen and then tripod with his head."

In the middle of Nellie's description of taking photographs and then having her camera taken away, two men walked into the café. Both wore miners' knit hats and digger jackets, as if they had walked out of the mine and into the restaurant. Their boots clunked on the linoleum floor. They grabbed a booth at the front with one of them giving a hard stare toward the sheriff and group. Moonshine stood up and uttered a low growl, baring his teeth.

"Moonshine, what is it?" Nellie leaned close to his ear. "He must recognize one of those men," she said. "I don't . . ." Then she remembered the two men walking across the river from her, the ones she followed. Knit hats and something about them that had told her they were miners. Digger jackets, like the men in the restaurant were wearing. She turned her head away and was relieved she had worn her own knit hat with her hair tucked inside. Maybe she looked like a small man with two big men. With her hand on Moonie's head, she could feel him gathering strength to attack, and she wrapped her hand around his collar. "No, Moonie. Not here."

The man who stared then stood and walked toward them. "That dog don't belong here."

The sheriff answered. "Not your business." Rosy half rose from his chair.

"Hey, Bones," the man called to the owner. "That dog is threatening me. Kick him out."

"Now, Willie, it ain't doin' no harm, and these customers have already ordered. Are you and Archie goin' to order anythin' more than a beer or coffee?" The owner was also the cook, and he had turned from a large grill behind a short wall to answer the demand. "And sit for two hours smokin' cigarettes?" He turned back to cooking, dismissing the complaint.

"If that dog so much as makes a move toward me, I'll kill him." He, too, turned away and walked back to the booth.

"You already tried." Nellie couldn't resist but kept her voice low. She kept her head down. "I think he's one of the men I saw walking along the river and must be one of the two who tried to kill me with their dynamite at the Crystal mine entrance."

Rosy and the sheriff looked at each other. "I'll get their names again from the cook before we leave," Charlie said. "Keep hold of Moonshine. I don't want a gun battle here in the restaurant. Are you armed, Rosy?"

"Nope. Don't believe in guns, 'cept for huntin'."

The cook arrived with the lamb stew they had all ordered for dinner. The men in the booth had left earlier, apparently thinking the cook threatened them, Nellie thought. "Who were those men?" she asked.

"Ah, just layabouts around here. Willie and Archie. They're transient miners, working for the highest bidders, then leaving with bills unpaid. I'm surprised they're back. Gem fired them a while back for missing too much work. They musta found work again, maybe up canyon." He left to bring back salt and pepper and tomato sauce. "Anything else? You all new in town?"

"Would they take odd jobs or work for the moonshiners?" the sheriff asked.

"I wouldn't be surprised. Anything for a buck except honest work, is my opinion." Bones leaned over to pet Moonshine. "Nice dog that. I used to have a black Lab. Got crippled up, and I had to put him down." The cook's long face grew even longer. Nellie thought she spotted a tear or two in his eyes.

"Oh, I'm so sorry. Dogs are such important animals to us. Moonshine has saved my life more than once."

The cook's face split in a grin. "Moonshine, eh?" He nodded his head. "Good name." He left to return to his grill, even though there were no other customers.

"Did I tell you that revenuer with the cowboy boots was in the union meeting?" Nellie asked Charlie. "He got my camera and dropped it out the window. I don't know if he was trying to help or to break it up." Sorrow settled again on her shoulders like a mantle. "I hope I can fix it."

Rosy worked on his stew. "Maybe the sheriff's office can buy you a new one," he suggested, glancing at Charlie. "Seems this was done in the line of duty." He sat up straight. "I forgot, I have your film." He pulled the filmback from the inside pocket of his jacket. "Do you want these now? Think you got anything?"

Nellie shook her head. "I don't know. I couldn't take the time to focus and make certain the lens faced those horrible men. I'm fairly certain I managed to get the scribe person." She took the filmback and turned to Charlie. "Can they stop a meeting like that? Doesn't the constitution say something about freedom to associate? I was spitting mad before I even took the photographs. After they tried to destroy my Premo, I was so angry, I could have shot one of them." She held out the filmback. "Would you hold this until I can get to the studio? I'm afraid to carry it."

Charlie placed the film in his jacket. "Hard to tell in this town, Nell. We'll report all this to the police, and I'll contact the federal marshal and see what he can do. The police may not care, as Gem Mining Company buys their cars and the ambulances. The marshal is more interested in enforcing the Prohibition laws, it seems." He pushed his empty bowl away. "I think we've done all we can about the moonshiners. I have plenty of information to turn over to the Treasury men, the revenuers. They can follow up from what I can give them—names and information about the local officials approving their 'fine by license' program. It doesn't appear to me that any one of them is getting paid off. All the money goes into the city and county coffers." He told Rosy about their investigations in Wallace and Mullan. "I don't think there is anything left to do there. I want to find who set off the explosion in the mine and dynamited below the Monitor—maybe intent on hiding the Crystal. The police asked if I—we—would continue to work on that problem. They know they aren't believed around here."

"They don't know about me, do they?" Rosy asked. "I think I might be getting somewhere underground, but if any of the miners and muckers down there knew I might be associated with the law, they'd shut me out faster than I could say 'miners on a pickle barrel.' "

"No, that is just between us three."

Nellie had finished her dinner, too. "Maybe we shouldn't be seen together. Those men might figure we are part of the investigation." She pushed her bowl away. "Are you paying, Sheriff? I have to take Moonshine out for a short walk."

Charlie stared at Nellie. "Alone? Do you think that is wise?"

Nellie attached the dog's leash. "I won't be alone. I'll have my dog." She left the café.

Moonshine pulled on his leash as Nellie walked outside. She chose a side road leading uphill to the boardinghouse, wanting to stay inside whatever light pools she could find. Maybe it wasn't wise. As she turned, she caught a glimpse of two men waiting in a doorway across the street. One held a gun. As Rosy also exited the café, Nellie shouted, "Help! Help!" She didn't want to use his name. Then Charlie hurried from the café, too. He caught up with Nellie. "I saw two men waiting over there . . ." She pointed to the doorway one up from the YMCA entrance.

The sheriff hustled across the street, but the doorway was empty. Where did they go? Nell asked herself. How could they disappear so quickly? Even Moonshine, whom she had released to chase after the sheriff, looked puzzled.

Charlie tried the door, but it didn't budge. He shrugged. "Locked. Are you certain you saw someone here?"

Nellie peered through the door and saw stairs leading up. As near as she could tell, no men climbed the stairs. Maybe there was another door inside that led into the YMCA. "I know I saw those two men—same knit hats and clothes. One of them carried a gun. I saw it. Maybe they had a key. Do you know what is up the stairs?"

Rosy joined them. "I know. There's some sort of meeting hall for Masons and such. One of the men talked about the group in the mine. They won't let Catholics join because they have to confess to priests, and there's a bunch of secrets they all keep." He shook his head and he, too, peered through the window in the doorway. "Being as how a lot of the miners are Catholics because they came from countries like Italy, Poland, and Croatia, seems kinda strange to me. Like carrying on their religious wars from Europe to here."

Nell and Charlie exchanged looks. Rosy didn't usually talk about philosophy or religion. "You're right, Rosy. What a keen observation to make. Now I'll have to think about it, too," Nell said. The three of them began walking up the street. They passed the Hope Studio. Nell stopped to look at the display in the window and sighed. "Wouldn't it be wonderful to have one's own photography business and studio, like this one?" This time, the two men looked at each other.

"Does the owner sell cameras?" Charlie asked. The dark kept all of them from seeing many of the photographs displayed.

"No, only photographs, mostly portraits, but most of the photos in the window have something to do with the mines—buildings and equipment around here. Inside, he has a display of portraits and weddings of some of his clients." She gestured toward the door. "No dead people as near as I could tell." She grinned and walked on.

"Did the Chicago store you worked in have photos of dead people displayed?" Rosy sounded truly curious.

Nell laughed. "No, those were just for family—my specialty, as it turned out." She placed each hand through the men's arms on either side of her. "Maybe now more of a specialty than I ever would have thought. Remember the Craters of the Moon?" She shuddered, sorry she had brought up that subject. She didn't think she could ever again visit the new national monument without thinking of their life-threatening adventures.

Chapter Twenty

Next morning, Nell left the hotel early with Moonshine and her damaged camera. She walked to the Hope Studio and was surprised to find it closed. "Now what, Moonie?" She decided to find a hard-goods store and see what kind of tape she could locate to patch the bellows on her Premo. There was no store on the same side of the street, so she crossed to the YMCA. Several men exited from the doorway where she had seen the men hiding. She greeted them and asked, "What does that door lead to? I'm new in town. Is it part of the Y?"

One of the men—she recognized him from the hotel as being a guest there—answered her. "It's the Masonic Temple. We had a breakfast meeting there. No women allowed, although I think there is a women's group that does meet here from time to time." He lifted his hat and replaced it. The other men ignored her, and they walked up the street. She wanted to go up the stairs, but didn't want them to see her do it. Then Walter Hope came out the door.

"Oh. I was looking for you, Walter. I need help with my Premo. Are you a Mason, too?"

Walter smiled. "Too? I don't think you are. You could join the ladies of the Eastern Star if you are interested in ladies' groups. Mickey seems to think they are all stuck up."

"Are the men in the Masons all stuck up?" Nellie smiled to take the sting out of her words. She suspected they were, secrets and all.

"Probably. I joined because it is good for business to know as many people as possible in town. There are several men's groups, and I belong to all of 'em. It gets to be a trial." He gestured to Nell to cross the street with him. "Let's go look about your camera. I can see it has suffered some indignities."

As Walter unlocked the door of his studio, Nellie commented, "I would think that most decisions about portraits and weddings are made by the women in the family. Don't you agree? So, being part of men's groups might not be helpful."

Walter sighed. "You might be right. Business isn't so good. We need more weddings around here. Or family groups, but those tend to be associated with the churches. I'm not much for church services, although sometimes the Masons seem more church-oriented than some of the established religious groups themselves."

"What do you mean?" Nell followed Walter into the storefront and placed her camera on the front desk. Moonshine sat near her legs and then moved up onto the shelf in the window.

"Oh, rituals and secrets. Special handshakes and recitations." He took off his coat and began to inspect Nell's camera. "I've probably said too much already."

"Do any of the miners belong to the Masons?" The men last night seemed much too rough to care about such things, but how would she know? Bootleggers certainly liked their secrets. Maybe rituals provided a relief from the hard and risky work of mining.

"Some mine officials and a few miners have joined. It seems there are always men who want to be in what they perceive to be an anti-Catholic group instead of a pro-Protestant organization. It takes all kinds, I guess." He poked around the bellows and the broken panel. "I think I can fix this up, but it won't be as good. Still, the exquisite craftsmanship of the wood is worth saving." Walter looked up at Nellie. "Fortunately, your lens wasn't scratched as near as I can tell. You can still use it."

Nellie sighed her relief. "I also have some film in this filmback to develop. When might I use your darkroom again? Also, the sheriff said I could pay you for that use. The photos are part of an investigation."

"Payment is always welcome, Miss Burns, although your help in some of my work has been payment enough."

Happy to be back in a darkroom, Nellie unloaded the film. She was much more experienced with developing one sheet at a time. The filmback permitted ten photos on one roll. She decided to develop at least two at a time, if possible. She would use fewer chemicals that way. Once again, as the photos began to reveal themselves, she felt the magic of the process and settled in to the pleasure of finding out each negative's strengths and weaknesses. The photos of the women at the bordello stood out for her, and she thought of each woman and the personalities they displayed. When she turned to the photographs of the union meeting intrusion, she fretted, uncertain whether she had captured anything worthwhile.

The company scribe, as she thought of him, was definitely worth the risks she had taken. His spectacled face, gray hair, sober face, and half scowl brought his presence right into the darkroom with her. The sheriff could take it to the company offices and find out who he was. The armed men were less clear, almost fuzzy, especially the tops of their faces above their bandanas. However, their clothes appeared in good detail. The only problem there was that nearly all miners dressed similarly. After the negatives dried, she printed one photo of each, knowing she could study them in more detail in her room.

The process of developing and printing took almost four hours. Nellie decided to first deliver the union hall photos to the sheriff. He had said he was going back to the paymaster's office to finish looking at the shift records. Rosy had headed to work in the mine, she was sure. Then she could visit the bordello to show the prints to the women and take orders for the final pictures.

Walking to the paymaster's office took little time. She knocked on the door and then opened it. And there sat scowly face himself. She doubted he could recognize her from the previous night as, today, she wore a dress and a fashionable hat and looked not at all like a miner, she hoped. "Is Sheriff Azgo here? I thought he would be reviewing your pay records."

"No!" The scowl deepened. "I sent him packing. Tired of all this folderol about who worked when and where and how much they made. None of your darned business."

Nellie was glad she didn't have her camera with her. He would surely have recognized her then. Maybe he did anyway, as he connected her with the sheriff. She cleared her throat. "I simply wanted to talk to the sheriff. He is doing the work of your own police department, I believe." She wanted to sound conciliatory, but it was difficult to keep an edge out of her voice. She heard footsteps down the walkway and glanced sideways. There he was.

"Sorry to disturb you, sir," Nellie said to the scribe. She closed the door and walked to meet Charlie. "Well, I have one question answered. That man in there is the 'scribe' who took names at the union meeting, albeit false names. His mood hasn't improved at all." She handed the prints to the sheriff, then turned to accompany him along the raised wood walk. "He said he sent you packing."

"*Humph.* I did finish what I started last night, no thanks to him." Charlie stopped to peer closely at the prints. "No question, it was the paymaster at your meeting. The other two pictures aren't so clear. Those men did threaten, didn't they?"

"The detail of their clothes is better, but I suppose they look like all the other miners in town." Nellie leaned over to see what

Charlie was seeing. "Maybe we should go to a place with better light"—she glanced up at the roof over the walkway that cast them into shade—"the café or the conference room at the hotel. We might see a detail or three to help us sort out the intruders from the run-of-the-mill miner."

"All right." He handed the prints back to Nellie, who placed them in her satchel. "I'm hungry besides. Then I have a meeting in Wallace with the revenuers to get rid of the moonshiner operation. Do you want to come with me?"

Nellie wavered. She wanted to deliver the photos to the women, but she would rather spend the time with Charlie. She also hoped to see who the revenuers were, especially the one with the cowboy boots who had seemed so interested in her. She had left Moonie in the Hope Studio's window and stopped to collect him as she and the sheriff walked back uptown. Walter said that Moonshine had again attracted at least one more customer into the studio, and could he keep him for a while longer. "That would help me, too," she said. "I'll come back later then, if that is all right with you. Any luck with my camera?"

"Not yet. I have been busy, but, before I close for the day, I will have some time to spend with it. Don't worry, Miss Burns. It should be working again by this evening." Walter saluted her as she left to join the sheriff.

Nell led the way into the county courthouse, an imposing building in Wallace. No longer dressed as a miner or even as a photographer, she still felt her difference from all the other people she and the sheriff met. They were all men. Even in the conference room where they gathered with the federal marshal from Spokane and several revenuers, she was the only woman. One of the men took notes. Nell might have expected to see a woman secretary, but no. The marshal looked half askance at her until the sheriff introduced her as an official photographer in the investigation of the Volstead Act offenses. After that, the marshal ignored her.

"My photographer and I have spent the past two weeks investigating the illegal bootlegging and sales of liquor here in Shoshone County, primarily in Mullan and Wallace, as requested by the federal marshal in Boise, Idaho. There were concerns about local officials and police, and so we were selected as independent from the legal establishment in the county." The sheriff sat on one side of the table and she on another. His voice was low, the cadence mesmerizing as he enunciated every word.

Nell listened as the sheriff described their activities—finding illegal stills, undercover visits to soft-drink parlors, the fine-by-license system, discussions with former police officers, and so on. The conference room was warm, and his voice droned on. She realized she had half fallen asleep when he gestured to her as his colleague and asked her to add her comments. It took her a moment to gather herself and the folder of photographs she had brought to present.

"Thank you, Sheriff. These photographs can confirm several of the sites we visited. The operations are designated by the locations—two from closed mine sites and two in the forests as listed. You may be able to identify the individuals. During our investigation, we also learned about the death of a bootleg operator."

A revenuer interrupted her—one she had not met. "We know about him. You were not supposed to investigate that—just the Prohibition violations."

Nell gazed at him a moment and continued as if he hadn't said anything. "We checked the county morgue records, which confirmed what an informant told us, that the man drowned. There was a question whether it was in a river or in a still." There was a rustle in the room, but, when she looked around, she could not tell who moved. She paused a moment, considering whether to say anything else and plunged ahead. "We could not locate a family. I do hope someone will have undertaken that responsibility to the dead person." The same thought occurred to her regarding the dead miners. Something else to investigate, but not here and not now.

Nellie routed the prints around the table, expecting questions or comments. One of the revenuers was the man who wore cowboy boots. She had noticed him when they entered the room. He avoided looking at her, but he studied the photos carefully. "Was this from the camera—"

"Yes," she interrupted, not wanting to get into any discussion of the union meeting or his part in it. Had he been a spy for Gem? No liquor had been present at the meeting.

The same man, whose name she did not know, added, "I helped Sheriff Azgo at one of the sites that's not pictured here, as Miss Burns was not on that foray. These photos do show the kind of operations we found."

The sheriff merely nodded. He didn't add, as he had told Nellie, that the revenuer had been little help and almost tipped off the bootleggers about their presence. The federal marshal, who wore a brown suit that matched his hair and mustache, merely nodded again and again. His face was pasty as a biscuit. When he asked a question, he directed it to the sheriff, not to Nell, even when it was about a location in a photograph. Nell figured she might as well have been a spot on the wall for all the good to be there, although the sheriff passed a couple of questions on to her to answer.

Charlie finally concluded their presentation. "We feel we have gathered all of the information we can. Our presence is now known in the two towns. We are investigating a different situation here in Bitterroot at the request of local police. When I return to Ketchum and Hailey, I can give you a written report. In the meantime, you have these photographs. We consider our work for the marshal's office in Idaho complete."

The federal marshal nodded again. "One more thing," Charlie said. He glanced around the room. "The man who found the bootlegger body gave his name as John Smith, undoubtedly a false name. Still, you might want to follow up, as drowning in a still does not sound like an accident." He stared at the cowboy boot revenuer, whose face had turned bright red. No one else said anything, so Nell and the sheriff gathered up their papers and left.

"Whew! I'm glad that's over," Nell whispered. "I wonder if they believed a single thing we said." They exited the building together. "Let's go get my camera from the Hope Studio." She turned to Charlie and touched his sleeve. "Do you really think it was a revenuer man who drowned the bootlegger?"

"Yes, I think so. He almost alerted the moonshiners at the Success Mine, and he didn't follow up on his end of the job." Charlie shook his head. "Remind me not to get involved with any more Prohibition investigations. We will probably never know what the feds will do with this one."

Chapter Twenty-One

When Nellie returned to Mimi's place, she brought the photographs she had taken of each of the women. Most were delighted. Several ordered additional copies, so Nellie's impulse to take the photos and give them to the subjects benefited Nell, too.

Mimi looked at hers and returned them to the envelope. "Are you coming to the town dance?"

"Dance? Here in Bitterroot? Is the whole town coming?" The idea of a dance appealed to Nellie, but what would she wear?

Mimi smiled. "Yes, here at the YMCA gymnasium. Not everyone comes, but many do—miners, mine officers. Some owners. Even I go, although most of my girls do not. They are not particularly welcome, and besides, they don't want to give up a chance to make money."

"What kind of dance?" Nell recalled she had been invited to a May Festival in Hailey by Charlie a year ago, but there had been no dancing.

"Mostly waltzes and two-steps." Mimi shrugged. "No square dancing, usually. Couples come, but also single people. It is a bit of an equalizer. We have two a year."

Nell wondered if Charlie and Rosy would go, or if they had even heard about it. "What does one wear?"

"Mostly dress-up, but this is a mining town, so no such thing as tuxedos and ball gowns." Mimi gestured to Nell's dress. "That would be suitable."

Nell looked down at herself. "This? Surely, something nicer."

"You would look lovely in anything you wore, Nell, except maybe work pants and boots—and then you would look like a man, which is probably the point of choosing to dress that way." She stood up from the chair opposite Nell. "Do come. It is tomorrow night. And bring that handsome sheriff with you. You could both use a lighthearted evening."

Nell wondered how much Mimi knew about her and Charlie's activities. She suspected quite a lot. "I'll think about it. I don't even know if Charlie dances!"

"He's Basque is he not? He dances, believe me." Mimi nodded her head and walked Nell to the door. "What else don't you know about him? Time to learn, Nell."

Nell felt as if Mimi were giving her motherly advice.

Nell persuaded Charlie to go to the dance. Rosy was harder to convince. When Nell and the sheriff left the hotel and walked to the YMCA, down Main and then turned left to go to the Y, she still didn't know if Rosy would turn up. It was just as well if they didn't go together. They still investigated the mine explosion and didn't want Rosy connected to them. It might be dangerous for him.

At the YMCA, people gathered and climbed the stairs to the front door. Inside, the smell of chlorine from the swimming pool almost overpowered her, but, as everyone moved through a short reception area and then into the gymnasium, the odor diminished. Forsythia branches stood in tall vases. Tulips and daffodils gathered in shorter bouquets decorated a front desk. Inside the gymnasium, pink and yellow crepe paper was strung in waves across the ceiling and hung in twirls down the walls. Nell could hardly believe how festive the room looked after the gloomy, gray days most of the time she and Charlie had been in town.

A small group of musicians—a piano, a saxophone, a drum, and a violin—played at one end as attendees began to fill up the large room. Chairs sat around a few small tables at the other end. A low bleacher provided three rows of seats across from the entrance door. The rest of the room appeared ready for dancing.

"Let's sit and watch a while," Nell suggested. It had been so long since she had attended a dance, she was nervous about stepping on Charlie's toes or Rosy's, if he decided to come.

"All right," Charlie said.

Maybe he was as nervous as Nellie was, she thought. They crossed to the bleachers and seated themselves at one end. Nell wore a lilac shaded dress, one she had stuck in at the last moment, just in case she needed to "dress up." Here was the opportunity, although not one she had really expected. She had thought more in terms of a ladies' club or tea. Charlie wore dark slacks, not Levis, a white shirt and a string tie. He fit right in with all the other men. The only difference was that he wore an embroidered vest in a dark red color with geometric patterns in pale red, green, and white. The Basque colors, she realized.

Couples began dancing to the music, generally moving in a clockwise direction around the room. Nell glanced at the door to see if she could see Rosy. Instead, she spotted Mimi accompanied by a handsome man, much taller than she, in a business-type suit. When he glanced around the room, Nell saw that his eyes were the bluest blue she had ever seen. His hair was light brown but with edges of gray around his face. Several people either waved at them or stopped to speak and then moved on. Before long, Mimi and her escort moved onto the dance floor. They moved in such synchronicity, they seemed glued to each other.

"I'm ready, Charlie. Let's dance."

He looked at her with speculation in his eyes. "All right."

Charlie led her onto the gym floor and placed his arm around her waist, and she rested one hand on his shoulder and the other in his hand. She had not been this close to Charlie, except on a horse, in a long time. Minus the day he saved her from the mud. She blushed, thinking about the bathtub.

The music was *Dreaming in the Moonlight,* a song Nell knew, a waltz. Charlie's hold was firm, and they swept onto the floor amidst other couples. She counted to herself. One two three. One two three, until she felt comfortable and then relaxed her shoulders and followed Charlie's lead. He definitely knew how to dance. She smiled up at him. He studied her and he, too, seemed to let his taut shoulders ease, and the smallest of smiles returned hers. Although shorter, she fit well against him. His cheek touched hers.

They swept around the room with the other couples. Nell recognized several people—Walter and Mickey, the revenuer man, Ira, Dr. Parker. Charlie, too, nodded to several men she had not met. Mimi and her escort appeared from time to time. At last, the band members took a rest. Nell sat on a bleacher while Charlie went back to the reception area to find them refreshments. She needed the rest. Soon, Mimi sat next to her.

"Does he dance?"

"Yes, indeed! You were correct." She faced Mimi. "Who is your escort? He is such a handsome man!"

Mimi blushed, which surprised Nell. "An old friend. We only see each other occasionally."

"Is he from out of town?" Nell wasn't certain how curious to be.

"No, he owns a mine near Burke. He rarely comes into Bitterroot." Mimi turned away briefly, then back and changed the subject. "My, you look lovely in that color, Nell. I am glad you and the sheriff decided to come. You can see this event is open to everyone. No conflicts allowed in here. Union members and mine officials all mingle on friendly terms. Most of the time."

A man Nellie did not know approached them. Mimi said, "Monty! I didn't know you might be here." Her voice and smile were warm. She stood and placed her hands in his, as he held them toward her. "When did you return to town? I see Dolly and Gordie frequently, as you probably know. Dolly didn't mention you might be back."

The man named Monty leaned over and kissed Mimi's cheek. "You look beautiful as ever, Mimi. Care to dance?"

The music had begun again, but Mimi's escort had not yet returned. She glanced around the room. "I would love to. I am here with Ben, just so you know."

The man gave Mimi a sad smile. "Yes, I thought that would be the case when I saw Ben in the foyer." He placed his arm around Mimi and swept her away.

Nell was left to wonder about Ben and Monty. She suspected there were stories to go with each name. Charlie came back and handed Nell a seltzer. Rosy was with him.

"Look who I found: Ross Kipling from Ketchum."

"Why, Rosy, what are you doing in the wild north? Are you working here?" She felt like such a fraud but followed Charlie's lead to protect Rosy.

"I've seen Pierce and Rinaldi," Charlie said. "I wish you had your camera, Nell. You could take some photos of all this activity. I would like to see who talks to whom."

"Same here," Rosy said. "I saw Rinaldi with one of the men the union considers to be a spy for the Gem. Pierce looks drunk. He has a flask in his pocket, but no one seems to care."

"Were they talking to each other?"

"Nope. The police chief is wandering around, too. Someone in the cigar room said he takes names and then takes bribes not to give a ticket or make an arrest. Don't know if that's true or not. Might be sour grapes."

"Hmm. Maybe I will go to the cigar room, except I hate the smell. Rosy, would you dance with Nell? I will return soon." And off he went.

"Do you dance, Rosy? We can sit here if you don't want to. I'm still catching my breath."

"Darned tootin' I do. C'mon, Missy. Let's show 'em how it's done." Rosy pulled Nell up by her hand, placed his arm around her and swung her onto the floor. She wasn't quite sure what step he was doing, but, like Charlie, he had a firm grip on her. The music sped up, and all the dancers whooped and hollered, Rosy among them. Nell tried to keep up.

They made one sweep around the room. "I have to stop, Rosy! I'm out of breath!" Her earlier ordeal had affected her more than she had thought.

The gym doors swung open, and two men dashed in, shouting. "Burke is on fire!" "Burke is burnin'." The music stopped. All the dancing ceased, and men began to gather at the doors. Nell noticed Mimi was back with Ben. He still had an arm around her.

"We need to get the fire engine and help up there now!" a voice in the crowd shouted.

Ben stepped forward. "Is the Hyperion on fire, too?"

"Don't know. Sounds like the whole damned valley up there is burnin' up!"

Ben turned back to Mimi and, right there in front of everyone, hugged her close and gave her a long, passionate kiss, the likes of which Nellie had never seen, nor experienced herself. Then he let her go and hurried with other men out of the gym.

A voice behind Nell almost shouted. "Well, I never. You know he's a married man! Acting like that in public."

Nell hurried to Mimi's side. "Are you all right?"

"Yes. And you? Here comes your sheriff!" Her face still carried a blush, or maybe a whisker burn.

Indeed, he pushed through the stream of men going in the opposite direction. "I am going up there. Do you and Rosy want to come? I have already arranged for an automobile."

Rosy still stayed near Nell. They looked at each other. "Yes!" All three left the Y. Mimi called to Nell, "Be careful!"

"I need my camera. Go by the hotel so I can check on Moonshine and gather up my equipment, please."

Chapter Twenty-Two

Charlie sighed and agreed when Nell returned to the automobile not only with her camera gear but also with Moonshine. He wanted to get to Burke as soon as possible. Maybe the fire was begun by the same people who exploded dynamite in the Gem mine. Leads to that disaster seemed chary at best. He knew at least half the room at the dance had left immediately to do what he, Nell, and Rosy, and now the dog, were doing—following news of a fire. He felt like a fire engine chaser. And, in fact, he was. A fire engine preceded him up the road toward Burke, red lights flashing and siren blaring. He followed closely in order to avoid getting into a line of autos heading in the same direction.

"Do you suppose it could be the same men who blasted in the Gem?" Nell asked. Half the time she thought the same questions he did. She should be his deputy and not just his photographer. Still, being a Basque sheriff in central Idaho was hard enough without naming a woman as an official law officer.

"I hope to find out if that is true," Charlie said. Rosy didn't offer an opinion from the back seat.

As their automobile neared Burke, they could see the red flare of flames reaching to the dark sky. Indeed, the whole canyon appeared to be on fire. A water wagon parked near the edge served two engines with hoses aimed toward burning buildings.

"That pissant of a stream ain't going to douse anything," Rosy said, pointing to the closest engine. "They need to get closer and access the creek, although maybe it's evaporated already. Damned hot in there." His face shone scarlet in the fiery light, and his hair almost looked as if it was catching fire.

"Scoot back, Rosy. We do not want to lose you. Walk around." Charlie gestured to the crowd gathering to watch the blaze. "See if you can get any news about how it began."

Charlie grabbed Nellie's hand. "You stay with me, Nell. We will go the other way. Moonshine . . . Please leash him. We do not want to lose him in the fire."

Nellie stooped and did as asked. Already, the heat brought out sweat on her face. Charlie wished he had discarded the vest he wore. First, it pegged him as Charlie Asteguigoiri, and, second, it was too hot. "Here," he said. "Don this vest so you will not get cold." It hung low on Nell.

"I don't think I will get cold, Charlie. It is so hot here, I am sweating all over." She did not reject it, however.

Small enclaves of men watched the fire, some edging closer than others. Speculation ran rampant. "Who started this mess?" "The whole town will burn. It's all wood." Heads shook. Charlie even saw a few tears running down men's faces. Not one other woman joined the spectators. Bringing Nell was probably a mistake. He remembered how she felt close to him while they danced. He wiped his forehead with a bandana. He could not be distracted.

The trio approached one of the fire engines, where a hatted man and uniformed man, probably a chief, directed where the hose should point. "Anyone know how this began?" Charlie asked.

"Who are you? And stay back! These buildings are beginning to fall!"

Charlie flashed his badge. He didn't give the man time to look carefully at it. True to his warning, timbers crashed, and the whooshing sounds of the flames and snapping wood turned the town into a holocaust.

Moonshine jerked on his leash, escaped Nellie's grasp, and ran toward the back side of one of the buildings not yet engulfed in flames. "Moonshine!" Nellie screamed and scrambled after him.

It took Charlie half a minute to gather himself to follow her. Even the man who had warned Charlie leapt forward. Neither was as fast as Moonshine or Nellie. The two of them had disappeared around the back side of the buildings. Charlie was frantic. If the front of the burning frame caved in, the rear could easily fall backwards. "Nell," he called. "Where are you?"

He listened, but the roar of the fire covered any response. Then he heard the faint sound of a dog bark. "Moonshine! Come!" He knew Rosy could make the dog come to him, but his own voice would be ignored, unless Nell heard him, too. He felt as if a vacuum was sweeping him toward the flames. The heat grew and pulled at him. What was it doing to such a slight woman as Nellie?

The fireman stopped, turned, and dashed back to his engine. Charlie kept scrambling uphill, stumbling and falling once, but continuing on, trying to catch up to Nell. For a small woman, she moved fast, but, of course, she would not let her dog burn. The fire continued to roar through town, but, where Charlie hustled, the air felt slightly cooler, maybe because all of the buildings at the beginning had now fallen victim to the flames. Even the sound diminished. Then the sheriff saw a creeping trail of fire in the brush running uphill. The fire was not only going to destroy the town, it might make a conflagration of the woods around it. He took a deep breath to quiet the panic he felt, called for Nell and Moonshine again, and leaped forward and up. A faint response, a woman's soprano, spurred him on.

Moonshine's leash had been around Nellie's left arm, her weak arm. When he pulled and dashed away, she couldn't stop him. "Moonshine! Come back!" She tried to rush behind him, but she soon lost sight of him. The ground sloped up, and bushes covered the hillside. Even as she felt the air cooling a little, the roar behind her frightened her into jumping over rocks, skipping around tangled brush, slipping in her hurry to catch her dog.

A roof on fire slid toward her as a building caved in. Embers dropped everywhere, and she felt the heat of one in her hair. Frantically, she brushed her hand across her head, down to her neck. A sharp nick of pain near her thumb told her she had brushed it off, but her head still felt as if her hair were sizzling. She grabbed a handful of dirt and spread it around her head. Moonie! she screamed inside. Don't burn up! Nellie dodged down a small gully, and her foot slapped into water. She ducked toward it, splashing snowmelt on her face and hair. Then she heard a man's voice calling.

"Charlie, Charlie. I'm over here!" Nell stayed near the water. She called for Moonshine again. "Moonie, oh Moonie!" She saw what appeared to be a flash of light coming toward her. As it neared, she realized it was Moonshine's teeth and eyes, reflecting the fierce fire above them. He carried a man's shoe in his mouth. "Oh, no. Is someone up there?"

Moonshine sprawled against Nell and then jumped up and took two steps up the side of the gully. He dropped the shoe and barked. Nell knew she should follow her dog to see if someone were injured or dying. Her muddy feet could hardly gain a foothold. And then Charlie entered the gully, too.

"Moonshine has a shoe and wants me to follow. Someone is up there!"

"You go back down, Nell." She heard his foot slap in the water, too. "Stay in the water. I'll go! Are you all right? I smell burning hair."

"It might be Moonie. Embers flew all over the hillside. I wet my head, so if it was burning, it isn't anymore. Hurry!"

Charlie scrabbled up the gully side. At the top, his form was backlit by the burning buildings. Another crashed to the ground. Nothing was going to stop the fire's progress through the town of Burke. Even the mines up the canyon would burn. Soon, the sheriff disappeared, and then Nellie worried flames or embers would swallow him. "Charlie, come back!"

The grass and brush near Nell caught fire, and a burning line moved uphill like a fuse leading to dynamite. What should she do? Try to get help, or chase after dog and man? The wind whipped around the burning town, creating its own firestorm. Within minutes, the whole hillside burst into flame. She couldn't wait any longer. Surely, Charlie and Moonshine could move farther out from the fire and return that way. She followed the gully down, half wading in the small creek. It wasn't deep enough to sink into for protection, but she scooped water onto her head, face, and dress, hoping that would protect her from a fiery death.

The gully spread out and disappeared. Still, the creek ran downhill. As soon as the heat dried her off, she splashed more water on herself. She felt singed hairs on her head and tried to sink her whole head into the running water. Then she shook herself like Moonshine and widened her steps downward, barely keeping her balance. She focused so intently on her feet, she ran right into Charlie. He grabbed her and held her tight. Moonshine jumped on her back. Relief speared through her.

"Did you find anyone?" Nell asked. She hoped no one died, but she was so relieved to have her man and her dog safe, she wept.

"Are you hurt?" Charlie moved his hands around her, feeling for injury.

"My hair is singed. How about you?" Nell wiped her face,

spreading mud around.

"I found two gas cans, a half-burned man, and a still-flickering torch. This was arson." He motioned to his feet. "One can is with me. I could not carry the man. He was dead and too hot to lift." He half lifted Nellie. "We must get to the bottom and back to the fire chief." He carried more than walked her, and the dog followed.

The fire had moved on from where only a few left of the crowd watched. The fire engine sat higher up the street, its small stream fighting a losing battle with the still roaring blaze. Another engine with a larger hose appeared to douse a few of the flames, but the town still burned. Charlie left the gas can with the fireman and gestured uphill toward where he had come down. They talked a while, and then Charlie helped Nell and Moonshine both to their automobile. "I told him where to reach me. They are too busy to talk now."

Nell curled around Moonshine and held Charlie's arm as he shifted, turned the auto around, and drove back to Bitterroot. She wept as she thought about how close a call it had been for all of them. Out loud, she wondered where Rosy was.

"He left. He told the fireman he found another way back to town." Charlie stroked Nell's head. "Sleep."

Chapter Twenty-Three

The café next door to the hotel cleared out after breakfast, except for Charlie and Rosy, who met to talk about the fire the night before. Nellie had dashed off to see Ira at the boardinghouse and asked them to wait for her. He had left an urgent message for Nellie at the hotel. She met briefly with him at the boardinghousee in the main dining room when no one else was there.

"Miss Burns, I heard there's another explosion planned in the mine. This one might be even worse and close down the mine. At least that's the aim."

Nellie knew rumors flew all over town about all sorts of bad happenings, especially after the fire at Burke. It seemed a firebug was on the loose, except one had already died. "Did you hear this in the assay office?" It seemed an odd place for rumors to land. More likely, a miner in one of the stopes would have heard it first and then passed it on.

"No, I heard it . . . somewhere else." Ira blushed from the roots of his hair clear down his neck.

Trying not to smile, Nellie decided not to ask where. It was probably at the brothel, Mimi's or maybe another one. "Do you think it is reliable?" From what she gathered during most of her conversations in the town and in Wallace and Mullan, any good story also made a "true" rumor.

"Don't know. Hate to think it's ignored, though. Just like last time, I heard the target is the main shaft, and it's going to happen on the graveyard shift, maybe tonight." Ira had removed his hat when Nellie joined him. Now he put it back on. "You might wanna alert the authorities, either at the mine or with the police. They won't give me two minutes of their time. I'm just a lowly miner." Ira made as if to leave, then sat again. "I remembered something else. I told you I thought someone else was in a drift getting out late. The reason I thought someone else was there was I heard what sounded like someone stumbling and then coughing. Like I said, I didn't see who it was." Other men came into the dining area, so Nellie left with Ira and headed back to the hotel.

Charlie and Rosy didn't appear to be talking when Nellie arrived, but she would fix that. Without more than a quick preamble, she told them what Ira had said, both about the possible explosion that night and his recall of the noises he heard.

"Makes no difference to me anymore," Rosy said. "I'm gettin' out of here. This hellhole is too dangerous. And you two should come with me. I'll take Moonie back with me anyway, so he won't get in no more trouble."

"I agree with you, Rosy. But we still do not know who set off the mine explosion. I told the local police we would help investigate. I cannot leave without at least some clearer path to the answer."

"And I am not leaving until Ch—the sheriff does." Nellie didn't bother to use being the official photographer as an excuse. She did lift her hand to her hair where she could feel the chopped off spot that had been singed.

"Nell, you should go with Rosy and Moonshine. You have been in danger too much. Time to leave." The sheriff didn't look at her.

"No." Nellie didn't feel quite as firm as she hoped her voice sounded. Maybe she could persuade Charlie to leave, given a day or two, but she believed Rosy was right to go. She was sure his boys missed him.

The three of them were silent for several minutes.

Finally, Nellie spoke up. "I trust Ira. He must believe another attempt to close the mine will happen. He has been forthcoming to me with his suspicions. Mimi thought he suspected Harry Pierce might have a hand in it."

"Pierce! You have not told me that."

"I just learned it a day or so ago, and we've been busy." Getting ready for the dance, she didn't add. "Sorry." She felt her cheeks grow warm.

Rosy laughed. "You two. Glad I ain't young no more."

By then, the café was empty except for the waitress at the far end of the counter.

"I have an idea," Rosy said, leaning close and lowering his voice. "I don't think either one of you will take to it." He glanced over his shoulder and back. "It involves Charlie and me going back into the mine, say, with the graveyard shift and snooping around. That'd take some pull from a super, though, and doesn't sound like it should be Pierce."

The sheriff frowned, and he pulled on his ear lobe. He was taking Rosy's suggestion seriously. He rubbed his cheek with the hand that looked singed from the fire. Nellie cringed but kept silent. She was afraid if she protested, that might encourage both of them to go ahead.

Rosy stood and took his coffee cup to get a refill. "Think about it," he said.

Charlie looked at Nell. "What do you think?"

Nell was surprised he wanted her opinion. Or maybe he just wanted to argue about it. "I'm not sure what you and Rosy could do in the mine to stop it. How would you know even where to go?"

Charlie nodded. "Yes, you are right. We would need someone who knows the mine well, the possibilities, the places where dynamite might be stored or who would have access." He pulled his hand through his thick, black hair.

A few more gray hairs seemed to appear. Oh dear, she thought. He is really considering doing this. "How about that man who took you on the tour—something Rinaldi?"

Rosy stood behind his chair. "The lead? Sure, he would know most of the ins and outs. Sounds like a know-it-all half the time. Those kind are all talk, usually, but I'd say he'd be a good choice." He moved around his chair to sit down and sip from his cup. "How would you go about fixing that up?"

"The local police Chief Turner has some pull around the mine, I believe. I can talk to him. See how to contact Rinaldi. Are you willing to do this, Rosy, if I can swing it?"

"Count me in, Carlos!" Rosy grinned.

Nellie looked from one to the other. They weren't going down there without her. She had all day to convince Charlie, and she could arrange for Moonshine to stay with Mr. Hope. "That's settled then," she said. "Let's go find Chief Turner, Charlie."

The sheriff and Rosy exchanged frowns.

"Guess you got your marching orders," Rosy said. "Let me know what you can figure out."

Chapter Twenty-Four

Nell and the sheriff walked with Rosy to the trains heading into the mine for the graveyard shift. She hoped no one would question her. She was back in her miner's dress—pants, jacket, hat to cover her hair, and boots—and had patted her cheeks with dust from a pile on the way up to the entrance from the main street. They had decided Charlie would load on a different rail car than the other two. A moon tipped near the western horizon, its light so bright it turned the valley into a silver village, mimicking the lodes underground. A miners' moon, Nellie named it to herself. She wondered how many miners missed the moon—working all evening or all night. And did they care? Rosy and Nell sat at the end of one car with Nell shielded by Rosy's size at the tail end. He said a few words in greeting, but Nell kept her lips shut. Her voice was a sure giveaway.

Chief Turner had contacted Buddy Rinaldi, and he and Charlie met with him. Charlie told Nellie and Rosy that Buddy had acted a little strange, maybe too eager. It had taken several hours for Nellie to convince Charlie to allow her to go with them, and mostly it was because she insisted and wouldn't stay at the hotel. She took Moonie to the photography studio and left him there.

The ride into the mine felt almost as urgent as the ride on the morning of the explosion, when everyone was in a hurry to get to the disaster. Her ride the day Harry Pierce took the sheriff and her to photograph and inspect the detritus of the explosion was much more leisurely. Lights were few and far between, but Nell could see portions of the tunnel, water dripping down, and a myriad of pipes and wires along the sides. She wished she could ask what everything was for. Another engine with one more car followed behind hers and Rosy's. This third trip into the mine seemed easier than the earlier ones, even though their goals might be deadly. She wondered if Charlie felt the same way. This was his fourth or fifth trip.

Charlie and Rosy decided to warn Gem Mining Company—not Harry Pierce but the general manager. And they also decided to go into the mine. And here they were. The trip on the man cars took twenty minutes to reach the main hoist room. Buddy Rinaldi met Charlie when he jumped off the car behind Nellie and Rosy. She wished she had Moonshine with her, but that had been impossible. He could smell out the bad people, or at least a burning fuse. She sighed. That would not have been smart, either. Moonie might be killed, and so might the three of them.

The men from the cars lined up by the shaft to ride a sled to go down to their work stations. No one seemed to be paying attention to Rinaldi as he talked with Charlie, and Rosy and Nellie hung back. A man not dressed like a miner talked with each miner as he loaded onto a sled. That must be the Pinkerton detective hired by the mining company, Nellie thought. She hoped the company had given him their names, although she wasn't certain who even knew they were heading into the mine. She decided to eavesdrop on Charlie and Rinaldi.

"We'll begin at Level Ten," Rinaldi was saying. "If the intent is to close down the mine, the closer to the main entry the better for the plotters." He kicked at a small pile of dirt on the graveled floor of the shaft room.

Lights cast shadows around the space, making it seem

brighter than it had been the first time Nellie came in. Maybe it was the contrast with the black ride inside the tunnel.

"Does every shaft station have a shed that can hold dynamite or disguise what someone is trying to do? It seems one of the miners was able to spot a man running from the shed before the last explosion." Charlie glanced around, maybe sensing Nellie was close by. He gave a short shake of his head. She took it as a warning to stay away, so she wandered back toward Rosy and didn't hear Rinaldi's answer. Still, he had said Level Ten.

"Let's go, Rosy. That man with Charlie said they would begin with Level Ten. Do you know how to get on the right sled?" Nellie was not at all sure she wanted to go deeper into the mine again. Already, the same as on the day of the explosion, the mountain felt like a huge burden over her head, a weight of minerals, soil, timbers, and trees. She straightened her shoulders as if in counterweight.

"Any sled is the right one, as long as we call out the level to the operator. Looks like the Pink is checking off men. Not sure how he's gonna take you." Rosy grinned. He had worn his patch for several days but no longer had it around his head and eye. "I can talk him up. You scoot onto the pickle barrel like you own it. Keep your head down. At Level Ten, jump off." His scarred eye caught the light and seemed to look right through Nell.

"You're coming with me, aren't you?" Nell grabbed Rosy's arm. She could feel his strength through his shirt. She wanted to stay close and borrow the confidence he always exuded. He and Charlie. She took a deep breath, shrugged her shoulders again as if to throw off the mountain, and walked toward the shaft and cable.

Rosy caught up and stayed next to her. They waited for the sled, and soon it appeared rising from the depths, not quite noiseless, but not noisy either. Nearly all the men had already descended to their work stations. Rosy stopped at the Pinkerton man, pointed to his eye, and made a joke about keeping an eye out for detectives like him. "Did you hear the one about the . . ." he said and lowered his voice to tell a story. The detective leaned over to hear Rosy.

Nell heard the word "prostitute" and shuddered. She climbed over the low side of the sled and sat herself with a thud on the perch, scooting to make room for her companion. Rosy kept talking and gestured with his hand to his eye. He ended with the words "I'll keep my eye out for you!" He rasped a low laugh and climbed in next to Nell. "Level Ten," he shouted to the loader. The detective sported a big grin and probably laughed, too, but the sled began to descend, and Nellie turned her attention to the front. She wanted to grab Rosy's arm again but thought the few men behind her would think it strange.

The pickle barrel, as Rosy called it, gathered speed. What if the cable broke? It took all of Nell's willpower not to cling to her friend. She closed her eyes at first but decided that was worse. If they were going to plunge to the bottom of the shaft, she wanted to know. Giant timbers over her head held the mountain in, out, up. After a short length, the sled slowed. The narrow shaft opened to a station. Level Ten, she breathed to herself. She was certain she would not be able to go any deeper. Rosy climbed out, and Nell stumbled after him. How did the cable operator know exactly where to stop? He was several hundred feet above them and completely out of sight. No matter. He knew his job well. Nell took another deep breath.

The sled continued down but soon slid up again, empty. Nell and Rosy waited. No one else stood around Level Ten. Nell began to relax a little. Soon, Charlie and the other man arrived on the sled and joined them. The sheriff introduced Rosy but again referred to Nell as Cord. She grunted, she hoped in a bass tone. They first investigated the small enclosure that served as the shaft station. It contained scalers, as Rosy called them, a drill, a number of drill bits, used candles, and little else. "Supply shack," Rinaldi offered. "Nothing unusual here." He gestured with his head toward a dark tunnel. "Let's go to the closest stope down this drift. Empty right now. No dynamiting today, so no muckers working. Still, the dynamite for any job has to be stored somewhere. Several stopes played out on this level." He gestured to the candles. "Take a couple. The electricity might not extend into the stope."

Charlie helped Nell get her carbide light burning so she could watch her step. The shifter had already headed along the drift, so she didn't feel awkward about the help. "How do we know he isn't the bad guy?" Nellie whispered to Charlie. Rosy talked to Rinaldi several yards ahead.

"We do not, but we needed help getting in here, so I am taking a chance." He motioned to Nellie with a finger in front of his lips.

Nell followed Charlie, and finally they all arrived at a timbered hole in a niche in the ground. The hole was maybe three feet by three feet and surrounded by wood. Nell could see the top of a ladder with wood steps. Uh-oh. She didn't think she was going to like this at all. Rinaldi swung himself onto the ladder and began descending. Rosy followed once Rinaldi himself was out of sight, although a faint glow from his carbide light could still be seen as she peered over the edge. There was no apparent end to the black below. Were they digging to China?

"I will go in front of you, Nell. Keep your face back and your hands on the sides. Otherwise your light may burn you." He, too, swung onto the ladder and stepped down a couple of feet. "If you have trouble, and you should not, I will be right below you to help. Do not worry." He patted the top step.

Nellie mimicked him in her head: Do not worry. She had been worried from the moment she and the others had unloaded from the man car—whether she'd be discovered, whether they could find new explosives, whether she could keep up, whether this was one of the stupidest things she'd ever done. Now she had to worry about climbing down in a hole in the ground like a gopher or vole. Or worse, losing her grip and falling.

She kept expecting the ladder to end, but it didn't. Down and down, step after step. Her hands ached from grasping the ladder sides. She called quietly down to Charlie. "How deep are we going?" There was no answer, and then a step under her boot cracked, and she almost lost her balance. Nell clung to the ladder sides and stopped, unable to force herself to step down again. Charlie's head appeared below her. "I can't do this anymore."

"You can. One step at a time. We should reach the stope in no time at all. I cannot see Rosy's light anymore."

Nell began her slow descent again.

Charlie waited for her at the bottom. "Here you are. That was not so bad, was it?"

Nell wondered if he was reassuring himself. It was bad. "Now what?"

"Rosy and Rinaldi have moved into the stope to see if any dynamite is being stored there." The sheriff pointed to the black around them.

Two faint lights moved back and forth in the Stygian darkness. Nellie was thankful for her carbide light, even if she had scorched her hands once or twice when she leaned down to see if Charlie were right below her. He always was. Charlie took her arm and guided her toward the two men. Their own lights seemed bright in comparison. Nellie could see the rock walls, the dirt floor, the timber sets holding up the ceiling. Nothing gleamed like silver or gold that she could see. Probably lead didn't glow. She felt a shift in the air.

"Charlie, I am going to stay here near the ladder. This doesn't feel right."

The sheriff shrugged and said, "All right. Suit yourself. I will see if they are finding anything of moment." His light measured his progress in the mined-out stope.

The rock surround felt as if it were a tunnel, which it was in a way. The miners followed veins of lead and silver until they ran out or disappeared going down or up. Rosy had explained some of the mining terms to Nell as they sat in the man car. Muckers shoved the rubble down chutes to the next level, where it was held until a skip-tender came along to release the night's work into ore cars.

Nell regretted not following Charlie to see what the end of a stope looked like. She doubted she would ever get another chance. Still, this was similar to the Triumph mine, where she and Rosy had visited miners working—drilling and setting "giant powder" as Rosy always called it. Maybe all mines were the same. This mine seemed much warmer, though. As she stood and listened, she could hear the faint voices of the men as they talked. Maybe they had found something.

Nell sensed the air shift again, and then the ground under her feet lurched sideways. Dust filled the air in the direction she was looking. She grabbed the ladder and climbed two steps. A man came running from the back of the stope—Rinaldi. Silence.

And then the mountain cracked.

Chapter Twenty-Five

Charlie shuffled his way to Rosy and Rinaldi near the back of the stope. He didn't feel any more comfortable than he had when Rinaldi showed him around and demonstrated what the miners and muckers were doing. It still felt as if the mountain above weighed him down. He thrust his shoulders up and back, defying his fears.

"Have you found anything?" Charlie was still getting used to averting the light from his carbide lantern so it didn't shine directly into the eyes of the others.

"An old drill and a scaler," Rinaldi answered. "This stope hasn't been worked for a while." He backed off from where he was standing and added, "And this."

Charlie came forward to stand by Rosy. The "this" was a half box of dynamite. Fuse cord wrapped in a circle lay atop the long cylinders wrapped in paper. The three of them looked down. "I guess the question is, was there another half, and, if so, where has it gone?"

Rosy knelt and tilted the box in different directions. "Might be a date on it." On one flap he discovered a notation of a date, one about seven days earlier but after the mine explosion that the sheriff and Nell were investigating. "Guess it says this giant powder wasn't used earlier." He stood and scratched his head under his tin hat. "But maybe that was all that was left in this box in the supply room. Shouldn't be here, though." He glanced at Rinaldi. "Should it?"

Rinaldi didn't answer. Instead, he leaned over and picked up three or four sticks and the fuse cord, as if to inspect them, and backed up a few steps, and then several more.

The sheriff squatted to inspect the box. He didn't see any blasting caps. "Someone would need blasting caps to set these off, true?" He looked around and saw that the shifter had moved toward the entrance to the stope. Charlie couldn't see Nell back that way, but he was certain she was still there. He wondered what the shifter had in mind and worried his trust was misplaced.

And then the whole stope lurched sideways and knocked Charlie off his feet. A sound like a locomotive in close quarters accompanied a fall of rocks and dirt behind him. He grasped Rosy's leg and pulled him down. Without thinking, Charlie covered his head and face with one arm, pushed with his legs against the stope face, and jerked Rosy toward him.

"Rock burst!" Rosy shouted. "Hang onto your hat!" Rocks crashed and tumbled toward them. A whoosh of air doused both of their carbide lights. Their fuel dumped out.

The sound of falling rock continued for over a minute. Rinaldi could have been buried, or he could have escaped the worst of it. Nell! Charlie tried to scramble to his feet. He must find her, be certain she was safe. Rosy's bulk hindered him. "Are you all right, Rosy?"

A rumble sounded from the miner's head. "Dadblameit! Worked all those years at the Triumph and never had a rock burst!" He shifted away from the sheriff. "Leg got hit by one of those damned rocks. It might be broke. Can't see a blamed thing!"

Indeed, the black surrounding them made it impossible to see a hand in front of a face. Charlie couldn't tell how close the rocks were to the two of them, whether the dynamite box had been hit—no blasting caps, he reminded himself—or whether the rest of the stope was completely blocked off. He took a deep breath and almost choked on the dust. He could not see that either. "We have to get to Nell, see that she is all right."

"We may not get anywhere soon. I only have one leg that works." Rosy rose and pulled the sheriff up. "Mighta broken the other one," he repeated.

"Sit down again and let me see if I can tell." Charlie heard Rosy let himself down against the back rock wall, and he, too, crouched, feeling his way along Rosy's legs. "Which one?"

Rosy took the sheriff's hand and guided it to the lower part of his left leg. "Ow!"

"I do not find a bone sticking out, but it may be broken inside. Stay there. I have two candles in my pocket. I will try to get one lit. Here is one for you to light." Every sound seemed exaggerated as Charlie reached into his jacket pocket—the rustle of his jacket, the strike of a match on rock. He held a candle toward where Rosy's chest might be. Even the flare of the match gave him some idea of their circumstances. The stope no longer existed; it was filled with rock and dirt. Rosy was covered with dust so he almost appeared to be a ghost. His tin hat still sat on the top of his head, but slaunchways.

"You could go out on Halloween and scare the bejesus out of everyone," Rosy said with a short snort of laughter, confirming to Charlie that he looked the same. "Don't look good back that way." He waved at the pile of rubble. "Maybe we should call for Nell, see if she answers. And what about Rinaldi? I don't see him anywhere, although he might just blend in with the dust and piles."

"Nell!" Charlie called. He gestured to Rosy to join him. "Nellie!" Their combined voices seemed to die in the debris filling all but their small cave in the stope. With his lit candle, Charlie stepped closer to the rocks and held it high. He thought he could see a space along one side, so he edged closer and pushed himself up against the pile to get a better look. "Nell!" Maybe his voice would carry farther from that vantage point. He listened and called again. He and Rosy waited for a response. Charlie's shoulders slumped. If the ladder or the raise had collapsed . . .

Almost as a whisper, he heard "Charlie!" Nell's voice, not Rinaldi's. The relief he felt overwhelmed him. He turned back to Rosy. "I heard her."

The sheriff climbed several rocks to get a closer look at the space he thought he saw. The candle light did not extend far, but enough to see a black tunnel of sorts. He dropped down again and picked up the metal tool. "A scaler, you said. How do you work it?"

"Just like it sounds. It's for scaling loose rock and dirt from the headwall." Rosy pointed up. "Here, hand it to me. I'll show you." The miner, still sitting, held the tool with two hands and motioned the top of the metal stick as if he were scraping an imaginary surface. "I don't want to scale right here, 'cause it might bring down more muck."

Charlie grasped the tool and reclaimed it. He looked around, but this was all he had to work with. He clambered back up the debris, settled his candle between two rocks and shoved the tip into the black space. Nothing stopped his probe, so he pushed himself higher and stretched his body to extend the scaler even more. "It looks like we could move through this opening, Rosy." There was a brief rattle of rocks, but then everything stilled again.

"Charlie! Rosy! Are you all right?" Nell's voice sounded much louder than her initial whispery response.

"Rosy's leg is hurt. I am fine. Both of us are shaken up. No light except candles. Are you all right?" Charlie tried to inch his way closer to her voice, as if she were pulling him to her.

"Shaken up. My light still works. What should I do? I can try to get help at . . ." Her voice faded again. "I hate to leave you."

"Go to the shaft. Rosy. . . ." Charlie turned his head toward the miner. "Is there an emergency call on the bell?"

Rosy told him, and he relayed the information to Nell. "Is Rinaldi with you?"

"No." Charlie wondered if Rinaldi had been crushed by the rock slide. He had appeared to be near the raise when the sheriff last saw him. If he wasn't with Nell, where could he be? Distrust wriggled into his thoughts. Maybe he had climbed the ladders, and Nell missed him somehow. It was not a conversation he could carry on across the pile of rocks.

Nell heaved a huge sigh of relief when she heard Charlie's voice. Thank heavens! He and Rosy were relatively safe. But what if the rock burst again? She was certain that was what had happened. All the scary stories were true. The mountain didn't like all the men tearing up its insides. She had heard that the Gem Company had begun to fill up played-out areas with sand, which was supposed to cut down on what had just happened in her stope. But it wasn't hers. It was the mountain's. Rinaldi had shoved her off the ladder, so she had ducked into a niche nearby when the earth shook. That might have been all that protected her from the onslaught of burst rock. She clung to her shelter until all the noise of the slide stopped, and no more rocks seemed bent on filling in the stope. When she gathered herself and peeked out, she saw that the ladders were still intact as was the raise, although she could only peer up ten or twelve steps.

Even after she deciphered Charlie's instructions, she hesitated. It was so far up the ladders. What if Rinaldi was up there, waiting to break her head, her neck. What if? The next burst might close up the raise and squash her. She'd rather see if she could get through whatever Charlie was testing from his side. Except she had no tools at all.

All right, she thought. One step after another, and move quickly, just in case. At least her light was still lit. Grateful for small favors, or maybe a big one, she grasped the sides of the first ladder and lifted one boot after the other, trying to concentrate on holding tight and moving her feet up and up and up. She was tempted to count but didn't want to discourage herself. She would return. This time, she was more aware of the rock surround, the air tube running down the side of the raise, and the steps. Going up, she could see cracked wood and avoid stepping in the middle. The way seemed shorter this time, although Rosy or Rinaldi had said something about the floor of the stope being a hundred feet below the tunnel level.

At the top, Nell eased her head up, looking right and left and around. No one seemed to be there, but maybe Rinaldi was hiding down the drift. Nell pulled herself off the ladder. Now which way? It was so dark around her, a dense black. Had they turned right or left to begin the entrance to the stope? She closed her eyes, trying to picture how they had approached the laddered raise. They had not walked too far from the shaft station. Rosy and Rinaldi had strode in front between the tracks. She and Charlie walked side by side. The two men pushed their way through wind doors. That was it! She would explore the tunnel and find the wind doors and go through them. They would serve as a marker, too, for getting back to the right stope.

Her luck held. Her first selection led to the wind doors in half a dozen yards. She pushed on them. They didn't move. There must be an automatic door opener of some sort, like a track changer for a rail car. She glanced around, her carbide light shining, and found a metal lever in the rails. She hadn't noticed Rosy or Rinaldi pushing anything, but her attention had been on her boots and not tripping. She kicked at the lever and hurt her big toe. She tried to stand on the metal, but it didn't move. She decided to get on her knees and shove with all her strength. As she did, the doors opened. Nell rose up and hurried through them before they could shut on her.

At the shaft shack, she gathered two scalers, several candles, and matches. She turned around, trying to decide if there was anything else she could use, or if she could see Rinaldi. Only then did she seek out the bell, where it hung outside the shack on a thick wire cable with a fragile seeming string hanging down. Nine bells, quickly hit. She waited for a response. None came, so she did the quick nine bells again. This time, there was an answer. Now, she must give the level. What did Charlie say? Two dings to call the sled and two dings for Level Ten, the second level down. She waited. And waited. Where was someone? She wanted to get back to the stope, help pull rocks out of the way for Charlie and Rosy.

Finally, the sled came with a quiet whine. In it were two men, each holding a shovel handle with the business end extending down the sled. "What's up?" one of the men asked.

"There was a rock burst in one of the stopes." Nell gestured down the tunnel. "Two men are trapped." What about the shifter? "I think a third man is . . . She didn't know what to say about Rinaldi and kept her voice low, but hiding her soprano words rarely worked. Still, the men nodded.

"That burst traveled through the mine. Hoistman got a couple other calls before you called from this level. Sorry about the wait. Let's go see what we can do with shovels. Look deep did it?" This from the second man. "I'm Txomin. Who're you? This here's Tater."

Nell tilted her head up, so Txomin could see her face. She lowered her voice as much as possible. "Cord." She could see recognition spark in his eyes. She pulled her hat down again to hide her face.

Tater asked, "That's an empty stope along here. Why wasn't

it filled with sand?" He shook his head. "Gem wants to kill us all."

Nell was surprised Tater was out of the hospital. He seemed fine—no bandages, no limps as he walked along. His voice sounded gravelly, as it had in the hospital. Maybe he suffered internal injuries. He did not recognize her, but he had been at least half sedated when she met him. She didn't remind him.

"First, they bomb us and now they crush us. Next time, it'll be another fire or somethin' else." He mumbled along as Txomin and Nell led the way.

The wind doors opened when Txomin pushed on them. Nell studied the rails and ground. She guessed there was only a lever on the other side. By the time they reached the stope, each carrying a scaler and the men still carrying their shovels, Nell felt warm, almost too warm. She motioned for the men to precede her on the ladders, which they did, handling their tools easily. She swung onto the wood steps with a little more grace than the first time, she thought, and descended as well.

In the stope, Nell showed the men where there appeared to be a passage along the top of the slide. She called out to Charlie. After several minutes, he answered "Here."

"I have help—Txomin and Tater, with shovels and scalers."

"Poke along the left side. May be a passageway. Push scaler through."

Txomin followed the instruction, and his scaler was not stopped by any rubble. He climbed up to extend his tool even farther and still no obstacle. "Looks that way to me," he called to Charlie at the other end. "We will dig to make it larger."

Txomin scanned the pile. He shook his head. "Charlie, we come for you."

Chapter Twenty-Six

Nell fretted because she could do little to help the men as they pushed, shoveled, scaled, and made their way to each other from opposite ends of the passageway. All she could do was worry about another rock burst, another slide. The sheriff had no experience mining, although maybe Rosy helped, too. She didn't know how badly he was hurt.

The two miners wore their carbide lights, so their work was illuminated. At last, Txomin said, "Looks big enough for a man. Can you come through, Carlos?"

For a moment, Nell was confused. Who was Carlos? Oh yes, Charlie. Being Basque had subjected him to discrimination. Having a Spanish name would have made it worse, she suspected. She shook her head while she waited to hear Charlie's response.

"I have wrapped my boot laces and jacket around Rosy's leg to keep it straight. I am going to lift him up and hope he can pull himself through with his arms." His voice came through well. "You will have to pull from your end, Txomin. Think it will work?"

Txomin shrugged. Tater asked, "Who is Rosy? We got ourselves another woman back there? No wonder the rock burst. Bad luck. In spades."

"Rosy is Ross Kipling. A miner who was with us," Nell said. "That is his nickname." She thought she should still keep their relationship a secret. Trusting anyone in this mine and out posed an obstacle to their investigation. Even if Rosy could get through the passage, how would he get up the ladder? There must be a way. Surely other hurt miners had been lifted out of stopes. She pondered going back to the shack and ringing for more help, a stretcher, or more men. She decided to wait for Charlie. One of the miners would know how to signal for what was needed, she hoped. They would need help to search for Rinaldi as well. Why did he run like that and toss her aside? Goosebumps lifted the hair on her arms inside her jacket. Something walking on her grave, her mother would have said. Was it Rinaldi?

A series of grunts and groans brought Nellie back to the reality of their situation. Txomin grabbed Rosy's wrists and pulled the man across rocks and dirt. When their joined wrists showed at the opening to the passageway, she leaped over to help. Tater pushed her out of the way. "You cain't do no good." He gestured with his head. Then he grabbed Rosy around the chest, and together the two men lowered him to the ground near the ladder. Rosy's face showed streaks of sweat and his cheeks signs of being scraped across rock, as did his arms where his shirt had peeled back. His grin showed white in his face blackened with dirt and debris. "Thanks, men. Now get Charlie to come through."

Even as he said it, Charlie's arms dropped into their space. Txomin stood to help him struggle the last few feet until Charlie stood up. Nell wanted to hug him but hung back. That certainly would not be appropriate behavior for a fellow miner, even if everyone had reckoned her to be a woman. "I'm so glad you are both safe and . . . well, at least Charlie is sound. How are we going to get Rosy up and out?"

The scrapes on both Charlie's and Rosy's faces oozed blood. Charlie wiped his arm across his cheeks, pulled out a bandana, and swiped Rosy's face. "Any water?" he asked. "I'll need my laces back to climb those ladders, Rosy." He squatted beside the miner. "How is your leg?"

"Hurts like hell," Rosy said. "But, I'll live." He gestured to the ladders. "Not sure how I'll manage my way out, though." He looked around. "Maybe I could use a scaler as a crutch if someone can push on my butt."

"That would be the fastest way," Txomin offered. "Otherwise, we got to wait for a stretcher crew to get down here. Could be a while."

While Charlie re-laced his boots, a rolling thunder spilled down the raise, causing waves of sound to push at Nell and the others. "What was that?"

"Sounded like dynamite to me," Tater said. "Bet another shack got blowed up, and this time, it's right on this level. We'll play hob gettin' out of here."

"Txomin, Tater, and Rosy, you figure it out. Come with me, Cord. I think we have our dynamiter dead to rights this time. He cannot get out either. We will find him." Charlie swung onto the ladder and stopped. "We need tin hats and lights. Txomin, hand me yours and add some liquid to Rosy's for Cord to wear." He donned Txomin's hat and light and began a hasty climb. Nell followed after securing Rosy's.

At the top of the ladders and in the tunnel, Charlie turned to Nell. "You go to the shack and see what you can see. Ring the bell if it is still there. Two dings, a rest, and two more dings."

"No, I'm coming with you. If the explosion was at the shack, nothing will be left, like last time."

"It is too dangerous, Nell. I almost lost you in the stope. I cannot afford to lose you." He pulled Nell to him.

She thought he was talking about her photography skills. But the hug meant more than that, she was certain. She circled him with her arms and held her face against his chest. "I almost lost you!" A few tears leaked from her eyes. "I'm coming with you."

They straightened up and let go of each other. "Then stay

behind me—all the way. If I get felled or anything happens, douse your light, get on the ground, and crawl in the opposite direction, in a hurry." Charlie squeezed her shoulder and stroked her cheek with his hand. "Let us go." He pulled on that long ear lobe of his.

No worry there. She was not that brave. Outfitted like a soldier, Nell followed in his footsteps. They turned toward the opposite direction from the shack. There was no electricity in what Nell thought was an old section of the mine. Either that or the explosion had destroyed the electric lights. A few candles were lit along the rock walls, but not enough. Their quarry might have lit them. Maybe his carbide light had failed.

Charlie's and Nell's boots slogged in muck where water had seeped down the walls. *Slap-oosh, slap-oosh.* The noise gave them no chance of sneaking up on him. The man they followed probably knew this mine like a rat knows its labyrinth. They did not.

Charlie stopped from time to time. The smell of sulfur would haunt Nell forever. She would no longer think just of hot springs or Ketchum, now so far away and safe. If the man could hear them, maybe they could hear him—and then they did.

At first, the *slap-oosh* sound was far away, like an echo of their own. Then it seemed to stop. Was he preparing another explosion like the first one or the one they heard a few minutes ago? In between were the horrible slide on the hillside when she nearly suffocated, the union meeting, the hospital visit, the men chasing them in Burke, the Burke fire—which of Dante's circles hadn't they visited?

The silence unnerved Nell more than anything. Charlie moved again, their shadows following like stalkers. When they passed through two wind doors, their head flames flickered and died. There were no candles beyond the doors.

Nell grabbed for Charlie and hooked her hands in his belt. "Now what?" Her voice came out somewhere between a whisper and a croak.

Charlie struck a match and lit his carbide light again and then Nell's. "I do not hear anything, do you?" Charlie asked. His voice sounded like a shout in the tunnel.

Nell shook her head. They slogged along again. When he stopped, there was deep silence except for dripping water. They rounded one more corner, and there the man was—sunk to his chest in quaking sands beyond a grid of metal. Buddy Rinaldi. He reached back toward them, his hands grasping like tentacles. "Help me!"

Neither Nell nor Charlie had a rope to pull him out. "Who helped you?" Charlie asked. He began a slow step across the grid of metal, edging forward, pulling off his jacket to extend his own arms.

"Help! Izzie did it." He thrashed and sank deeper. His eyes looked all white.

"He died in the fire," Charlie said.

Charlie leaned forward, but Nell held onto his belt with all her strength, and he stopped. Grotesque shadows danced on the cave walls. Rinaldi's head sank to the sand. Then, it covered his mouth and nose, and his eyes glazed. His hand groped above him. Less than a minute later, it was all over. The sands shivered and were still.

Chapter Twenty-Seven

When Nell reached the open air outside the mine, she was tempted to kneel down and kiss the train tracks. She had never been more thankful to reach a safe place. She knew she had stopped the sheriff from rescuing the shifter, Buddy Rinaldi. She also knew that it had been nigh on impossible to do so, and Charlie might have been sucked into the sands himself, and she could not have saved him. She wasn't certain Charlie knew the same facts. He had spoken so little on their way back to the stope ladders where Txomin and Tater were just getting Rosy out of the caved-in area to the main tunnel, she worried that Charlie was angry with her for letting a man die. Not only letting him die but stopping any chance of saving him.

As Rosy had hobbled along with the sheriff and Txomin mostly carrying him, an ore car pulled by an engine had come and taken all of them to the shaft. There, the dynamite set off by Rinaldi had not damaged the tracks. The blow instead had angled toward the tunnel itself, not as expertly set as the first one. "Rinaldi wasn't as skilled as he thought he was," Charlie said.

"He was all brag and no do," Rosy said. "He hung around a lot, acting like he was a supervisor instead of just a lead shifter."

"Maybe I can take his job," Tater said. "I can brag with the best of 'em."

A few timbers had broken and fallen in, but, with some effort, the men hefted Rosy next to the rail in the shaft to wait.

Charlie dinged the bell, which also hung unharmed, amazingly so, Nell thought. The string had burned, but Charlie pulled a hammer from his pack and gave the requisite signal. Shortly, the man-sled appeared, and all climbed in with Rosy.

Charlie and Nell took Rosy to the hospital, where Dr. Parker and Mickey plastered his lower leg. They daubed iodine on both men's cheeks where they had been scraped in the passageway out of the back of the stope. Rosy had several more bruises on his legs. Charlie's burn from the Burke fire appeared to be healing. Nell stood near the door to the emergency room, silent as a shade, while both men were treated. She had escaped any injury at all, for once. Her hunk of hair singed in the fire, she had cut off. The gap barely showed because she had combed the rest of her hair over the patch. A nurse handed crutches to Rosy and bid them all farewell.

Because the three of them had gone into the mine on the graveyard shift, Charlie had borrowed an auto again and driven to the changing rooms. Charlie then drove back to the changing rooms where the two of them picked up their clothes, and Nellie hung back. She had changed in her hotel room.

Rosy, leaning on his crutches, stopped to talk to several miners, explaining what they had been doing. "It wasn't the union who set off that explosion," Rosy said. "It was a company man—Buddy Rinaldi—and Izzie Savich. I think Izzie wanted to stop work so people wouldn't get miners' con. Rinaldi? Not sure what he was after—maybe to get union members in hot water." Men gathered around him, listening and then discussing among themselves.

"You're the new guy aren't you? What do you know about Gem and their doings?"

"Not as much as you. But I ain't staying around. My leg got busted in a rock burst. I'm heading out for a mine where a miner is treated better."

"Gem ain't so bad. You been up to some of the others around here?"

"No. I worked in the Triumph mine near Ketchum. We used water with our drills. No miners' con." Charlie picked up the clothes and listened. Nellie strained to hear all the comments.

Rosy continued: "You better join the union here, go on strike, and get better conditions. That's what I'd do."

They left, Rosy crutching carefully while he got used to the sticks.

They stopped at Bones's café across from the YMCA for breakfast. "It's time I returned to Hailey," Rosy said. "I wrote the boys, but they need me, and I need them. I don't want my sister to train them to be namby-pamby sissies."

"Or polite little gentlemen?" Nell hugged Rosy's arm. "Don't worry. I can see they take after you and their mother—adventurous, but sensible." She rolled her eyes at him. "Not that you are always sensible."

"Ho ho, Missy. Now look who's talking. Chasing after criminals to the Crystal Mine, up a burning hillside, and then mining underground!" He exchanged gleeful looks with the sheriff. "Are you gonna let her keep doing that kind of venturesome actions?"

Charlie pulled at his ear. "She does have a mind of her own, Rosy. I don't think anyone is going to settle her down, least of all me. I need someone strong and brave in my department. I think I'll retire you as a deputy until your leg heals and take her on."

"I'm sitting right here," Nell said. "Don't talk as if I'm out of sight." A deputy! Could she really do that? And what did Rosy mean, was Charlie going to "let her" do anything? He had no say over her, although if she was his deputy, he would. She didn't think the voters in Blaine County would accept a woman on the county's rolls as an officer. This was Idaho after all, not

Chicago or any big city.

"Speaking of getting back to Hailey, how are you going to make the long drive alone?" Nell asked.

"I thought mebbe you and Charlie here, along with Moonshine, would drive me home. I ain't never had a chauffeur type to do the driving. You drove my automobile all over kingdom come last summer, Missy. Maybe you could do it, and the sheriff here and I could rest in back, drink uh, soda, and rest up from all our wounds. All you lost was a hunk of hair!"

"It's a deal, Rosy. Of course, Moonshine would have to come along, too. He can sit in the front seat and navigate for us. Without him, we probably would never have discovered who tried to burn Burke down. That shoe identified him for sure. Mr. Pierce said the paymaster was the only man in the town who wore alligator shoes. Can you imagine? He must have been cheating on the payroll to afford something like that." She paused before taking her next bite. "Were they in cahoots with each other? Or were the shifter and miner separate from the Gem cheater?"

"You mean that SOB paymaster? And that dumb Croat and Rinaldi?"

"The paymaster must have had something on Rinaldi, or maybe they split the money they siphoned off the paychecks. Alligator shoes and Cadillacs," Charlie said. "I think Rinaldi stole parts and sold them to other mines. He took a handful of detonators the afternoon I was with him. And I thought he was supposed to be such a good guy," he continued. "Maybe these were all diversions to keep investigators busy." He shook his head. "Or blame the union miners."

"But what about the Crystal mine explosion?"

"Pure greed, in my opinion," Charlie said. "The Gem or maybe some of its officers wanted it hidden until they could get to it. Based on what I saw, it will be hidden for a long time."

Nell thought a moment. "Maybe. Seems like a strange way of going about it." She finished her plate and jumped back to the earlier subject. "And why Izzie?" Nellie asked. "Miners' con? If the mine was shut down, he wouldn't have to be inside for a while. Maybe he thought he would get better." Nellie turned to Rosy. "You knew him, didn't you, a little?"

"Probably his miners' con. He was almost dead from that! Think I'll get my paycheck before we leave?" Rosy grabbed his crutches. "Come to think of it, I better get down to the mine office and get my money before they forget I worked for 'em."

"I will take you, old man. You are not yet practiced on those crutches."

Nellie watched Rosy stand with his crutches. "Wait, Rosy. And you too, Charlie. I've been so relieved to escape from the mine, I didn't realize something important. Everyone connected with the first explosion and maybe the Crystal slide is dead, except maybe one: Rinaldi, Izzie, the paymaster. I think Izzie was one of the men on the hillside that morning. The other one? The man at the café?" She lowered her head, then looked at the two men. "I don't know who it was, but he must be in danger, too."

They glanced at each other. "He or Izzie almost killed you. Why do you care?" Rosy lifted a crutch and pointed it at Nellie.

"I don't know. I was probably where I shouldn't have been. But what if there is someone in the mine hierarchy who plotted all of this out? Should we stay to find out?"

Charlie grasped Nellie's hand. "No. I can tell Harry Pierce what we know or think, but we need to get out of here. You would be on that list, too."

"And so would you!"

Rosy shuffled to go, then stopped. "If I see any miners at the office, I'll say something. Not sure I care, Missy. You're alive, thanks to Moonshine and Charlie." He paused. "And your own courage. Thanks for getting us help in the mine!"

Charlie stood to help Rosy. "No. You stay here and take care of Nellie Burns. I'll take my time. Maybe come get me in a while to carry me to my room at the motor inn. I can pack then." With that, Rosy crutched himself out of the cafe.

The sheriff and Nellie sat in silence after Rosy left. Neither seemed willing to get up and return to the hotel. Moonshine surely needed to go outside.

"We—" Both spoke at once. Charlie gestured to Nellie to continue.

"We should decide if there is anything left to do here," Nellie offered. "Visit the police? Talk to someone else at the mine office? Maybe they can dig Rinaldi out of the sand trap?"

"Maybe we should decide where you and I go from here." Charlie's serious face turned to her, and he studied her. "I almost lost you, again." He still held her hand in his own. Nellie felt the roughness and his warmth. "Enough of that. You are too important to me." He inspected their hands as they rested on the table. He raised his face to look into her eyes. "You can be my deputy, or you can marry me. But probably not both."

Nellie felt herself blushing. The first woman deputy in the state appealed to her. All the close calls here in northern Idaho made her realize she didn't want to lose Charlie either. If he had fallen into the sand pit . . . She wouldn't even think of it. Then the second part of his sentence opened her eyes wide. She met his serious stare. Marriage? His proposal felt like a rock burst, completely unexpected. She valued her independence. Would marriage bury her like a ton of rocks? The planes and angles of his face had always attracted her. Maybe finally, she could take his portrait. And maybe being with Charlie always was exactly what she wanted.

"All right," she said, her heart filling with joy. "But you must understand something."

"As my deputy or as my wife?"

A thrill passed through her, and she leaned toward Charlie and placed her hands on his shoulders. "I intend to keep photographing, whether it is for you or on my own. Probably both," she said, realizing she was echoing him, but in the reverse.

"As my deputy?" Charlie's look turned into a tragic mask.

She shook her head, a small smile creeping up her face. "As your wife, dear Charlie, not as your deputy. I wouldn't want you to lose your position as sheriff at the next election. One of us has to earn a living!"

Charlie leaned toward Nellie and kissed her on the mouth. Nellie thought to herself, Now, I have experienced a real kiss, a deep, soul-satisfying kiss.

AUTHOR'S NOTE

Prohibition began in Idaho in 1916 and the rest of the United States in 1920 via the Volstead Act, passed by Congress as an amendment to the Constitution. My story in *Miners' Moon* deals with an era in Idaho when FBI agents and "revenuers" flooded North Idaho and in particular the towns of Mullan and Wallace to shut down the "scofflaws" who ignored the law. Donna Krulitz Smith wrote a master's thesis at the University of Idaho entitled "*It Will All Come Out in the Courtroom*": *Prohibition in Shoshone County, Idaho.* Thanks to Smith's thesis, I was able to learn a great deal of detail about this period in the area where I grew up. The thesis reads like a thriller in many respects. Unfortunately, Smith died in December 2009. A fellow writer, Ron Roizen, pointed out Smith's work to me, and I thank Ron. Although I fictionalized the story told by Smith, the general outlines of participation of moonshiners, city fathers, police, and revenue agents follow the truth as explicated by Smith.

The story of the mine explosion is complete fiction. However, the story about the Crystal mine has some truth to it. I did change the years of when the Crystal mine was hidden by a landslide probably detonated by dynamite on purpose. The Crystal has been reopened as a tourist attraction along Interstate 90 between the towns of Kellogg and Wallace, and I highly recommend a visit.

The town of Burke burned, but in an earlier year. Many of the outbuildings of nearby mines, such as the Hecla and the

Tiger-Poorman also burned. Burke never rebounded, although the mines did and operated for many years. The Hecla still operates from time to time.

ABOUT THE AUTHOR

Julie Weston grew up in Idaho and practiced law in Seattle, Washington. Her memoir of place, *The Good Times Are All Gone Now: Life, Death and Rebirth in an Idaho Mining Town* (University of Oklahoma Press, 2009), received honorable mention in the 2009 Idaho Book of the Year Award. Weston's mysteries, all published by Five Star Publishing, have won awards: *Moonshadows* (2015) was a finalist in the May Sarton Literary Award. *Basque Moon* (2016) won the 2017 WILLA Literary Award in Historical Fiction. *Moonscape* (2019) placed third in the Foreword INDIES Awards. Weston and her husband, Gerry Morrison, live in central Idaho where they ski, write, photograph, and enjoy the outdoors. Visit her website at www.julieweston.com.

The employees of Five Star Publishing hope you have enjoyed this book.

Our Five Star novels explore little-known chapters from America's history, stories told from unique perspectives that will entertain a broad range of readers.

Other Five Star books are available at your local library, bookstore, all major book distributors, and directly from Five Star/Gale.

Connect with Five Star Publishing

Visit us on Facebook:
https://www.facebook.com/FiveStarCengage

Email:
FiveStar@cengage.com

For information about titles and placing orders:
(800) 223-1244
gale.orders@cengage.com

To share your comments, write to us:
Five Star Publishing
Attn: Publisher
10 Water St., Suite 310
Waterville, ME 04901